A Note from Stephanie About the Dude of Her Dreams

A week in the saddle at a grubby dude ranch was not my idea of a dream vacation. Until I met Justin—my idea of a living dream. Justin was cute, smart, fun—and he liked me! I couldn't wait to spend every minute with this cute cowboy. But my dad had other plans. Like, lots of family togetherness—and no boyfriends allowed! But before I tell you more about that, let me tell you about my family.

Right now there are nine people and a dog living in our house—and for all I know, someone new could move in at any time. There's me, my big sister, D.J., my little sister, Michelle, and my dad, Danny. But that's just the beginning.

Uncle Jesse came first. My dad asked him to come live with us when my mom died, to help take care of me and my sisters.

Back then, Uncle Jesse didn't know much about taking care of three little girls. He was more into rock 'n' roll. So Dad asked his old college buddy, Joey Gladstone, to help out. Joey didn't know anything about kids, either—but it sure was funny watching him learn!

Having Uncle Jesse and Joey around was like

having three dads instead of one! But then something even better happened—Uncle Jesse fell in love. He married Becky Donaldson, Dad's co-host on his TV show, *Wake Up, San Francisco*. Aunt Becky's so nice—she's more like a big sister than an aunt.

Next Uncle Jesse and Aunt Becky had twin baby boys. Their names are Nicky and Alex, and they are adorable!

I love being part of a big family. Still, things can get pretty crazy when you live in such a full house!

FULL HOUSE™: Stephanie novels

Phone Call from a Flamingo
The Boy-Oh-Boy Next Door
Twin Troubles
Hip Hop Till You Drop
Here Comes the Brand-New Me
The Secret's Out
Daddy's Not-So-Little Girl
P.S. Friends Forever
Getting Even with the Flamingoes
The Dude of My Dreams

Available from MINSTREL Books

FULL HOUSE™
Stephanie

The Dude of My Dreams

Karen Bentley

A Parachute Press Book

A MINSTREL® BOOK

PUBLISHED BY POCKET BOOKS

New York   London   Toronto   Sydney   Tokyo   Singapore

A MINSTREL PAPERBACK *Original*

A Minstrel Book published by
POCKET BOOKS, a division of Simon & Schuster Inc.
1230 Avenue of the Americas, New York, NY 10020

A Parachute Press Book
Copyright © 1995 by Warner Bros. Television

FULL HOUSE, characters, names and all related indicia are trademarks of Warner Bros. Television © 1995

ISBN: 0-671-52274-4

First Minstrel Books printing June 1995

10 9 8 7 6 5 4 3 2

A MINSTREL BOOK and colophon are registered trademarks of Simon & Schuster Inc.

Cover photo by Schultz Photography

Printed in the U.S.A.

The Dude of My Dreams

CHAPTER
1

◆ ◀ ◆ ▪ ◆

"Well, of course we have to invite Brandon. And that cute friend of his, Ricky. And Jason and Dylan. And maybe that new red-haired boy from San Diego." Stephanie Tanner flipped her long blond ponytail over her shoulder, bit the end of her pencil, and frowned. "Does anybody remember what his name is?"

Stephanie's two best friends, Darcy Powell and Allie Taylor, both giggled. The girls were sitting in Allie's bedroom. An only child, Allie had the quietest house of the three, and they needed plenty of peace and quiet to plan their party.

They had started right after school, and they still weren't done!

"We can't *just* invite boys, Stephanie!" Allie pointed out. "Though, come to think of it, that's not a bad idea." Her green eyes shone as she grinned. "The three of us and a hundred boys at our first boy-girl party. What a history-making happening for us!"

Darcy gave a little snort, and Stephanie turned to look at her. Darcy was tall and slender, with shiny black hair and dark skin. Stephanie thought her friend was one of the prettiest girls in the whole junior high.

"No way," Darcy was saying. "No way would my parents ever let us get away with just invit-ing boys." She tapped her pencil on her pad of paper. "But speaking of parents, Stephanie, have you had a chance to talk to your dad?"

"My dad?" Stephanie repeated.

"Right," Allie said in her quiet voice. "Re-member, you said you were going to check with him about having the party at your house?"

"You *have* talked to him, haven't you, Steph-anie?" Darcy asked. "I mean, spring break starts in two days. So if we want to have this party over vacation, we'll have to invite kids *now*.''

"Um . . . um," Stephanie said. "Well, sure, I've *talked* to him." *I talked to him this morning,* she added to herself. *When I told him I wanted pancakes for breakfast. I just haven't talked to him about the party. Not yet, that is.*

"Terrific," Darcy said. "So we can call people and start inviting them this afternoon—just as soon as we figure out who to put on our list."

"Maybe we should invite those Flamingo girls," Allie said. "At least they talk a lot. I'm worried I won't have anything to say to the boys at the party."

Poor Allie, Stephanie thought. *Sometimes I forget how shy she is.* "We are not inviting the Flamingoes!" she declared. "We don't need a bunch of mean, stuck-up snobs to help us talk to boys. We have plenty to talk about on our own."

"But all the boys think the Flamingoes are hot," Allie argued. "Inviting them might make the difference between success or disaster."

"Well, I don't think we need them," Stephanie said. "Besides, if we invite them, all the boys will talk to them instead of us."

"Stephanie's right, Allie," Darcy said. "Remember, we're having this party so we can meet the boys of *our* dreams—not theirs!"

"I guess you're right." Allie smiled and clasped her hands together. "Isn't this just so majorly exciting?"

"Majorly." Stephanie sighed in agreement. She closed her eyes and tried to picture herself at her first boy-girl party. She was wearing a long, flowing black silk gown and sipping ginger ale from a champagne glass. Cool and poised, she discussed trends in modern art with Brandon Fallow, the Man of Her Dreams. Stephanie had always thought that Brandon, with his straight dark hair and dark eyes, was the cutest boy in school. He'd never paid very much attention to her, but then, most ninth-grade boys ignored seventh-grade girls like her. Anyway, Stephanie thought Brandon was Mr. Right and Prince Charming rolled into one.

In Stephanie's fantasy she gave a tinkling, silvery laugh and Brandon looked deep into her eyes. He took one of her diamond-ringed hands in his and raised it to his . . .

"Taco chips," Allie said, breaking into her

4

thoughts. "Everybody likes those. And maybe we should serve some of those little frankfurters wrapped in dough. What do you call those things?"

"Pigs in a blanket," Darcy told her. "My mom knows a really easy recipe for those, but you have to heat them up at the last minute. Steph, did your dad say it was okay for us to use your kitchen to make the refreshments for the party?"

"Um," Stephanie said. "Well, he didn't say it *wasn't* okay. So I guess that means it *is* okay!" As she spoke, a sudden guilty flush turned her cheeks pink. She turned her head away so her friends wouldn't notice, but Allie was too quick for her.

"Stephanie Tanner!" she cried. "You haven't even asked! You didn't talk to your dad about the party at all, did you?"

"Um," Stephanie mumbled, "well, I guess if you want me to be *strictly* honest . . . the answer is no. But I have a good reason!"

"This is unbelievable!" Darcy exclaimed. "You let us sit here all afternoon, getting totally excited about our first boy-girl party. And now we might not even have a place for it!"

"That's right, Steph," Allie put in. "This is totally unfair. We worked this out a long time ago. Remember? My house is too small for a party, and Darcy's parents are going to be away this weekend. You *promised* you'd ask your dad to let us have the party at your house! When exactly were you planning to talk to him, anyway?"

"Oh, sooner or later," Stephanie said airily. "But, trust me, in this case, *later* will definitely be better. *Later* won't give my dad time to go overboard and get all involved with our plans the way he always does."

"Maybe he won't do that this time. After all, we're older now. And lots more mature," Allie pointed out.

"True," Stephanie answered. "But he doesn't know that."

Darcy gave her a bright smile. "Then this is your chance to prove it!"

"Maybe," Stephanie said. "But I'm not sure he's ready for me to *be* grown up. He always says I can make my own decisions, but sometimes he just takes over."

"Maybe not this time," Darcy broke in. "I

mean, he let you decide how to redecorate your room. So now he's ready for the next step—letting you plan this party!"

Allie sighed. "Well, what *I* want to know," she said, "is whether or not we're getting to have the party."

"Definitely," Stephanie said firmly. "We are definitely having this party. My house, next Saturday night, rain or shine. I promise to talk to my dad about it tonight. And, now that that's settled, all we have to do is start calling all those boys!"

"And some girls, too," Darcy reminded her.

"Right!" Stephanie laughed. "Some girls, too. And now will somebody *please* hand me a phone? I'll start calling in invitations to the Party Event of the Year!"

At exactly 6:05 that evening, Stephanie slid into her chair at the big wooden table in the Tanner kitchen. With nine people in the house, there was always a crowd. Tonight, there were fewer people than usual. Stephanie's uncle Jesse was at the movies with her aunt Becky. Becky Donaldson co-hosted the TV show *Wake Up, San*

Francisco, with Stephanie's dad. Becky and Jesse's twin three-year-old sons, Nicky and Alex, were home, though. In fact, they had just spilled their milk all over the floor and were loudly crying about it. Stephanie's old sister, D.J., a high school senior, was baby-sitting for the boys. She was trying her best to quiet them down.

Joey Gladstone was busy mopping up the spill. Joey, a professional comedian, was an old college roommate of her dad's. He didn't seem to find the spilled milk very funny. Stephanie's younger sister, Michelle, was running to answer a ringing phone. Even with Becky and Jesse away, the kitchen was still crowded, confused, and noisy.

Meanwhile, Danny Tanner was busy at the stove. He flipped some cheese into a sizzling skillet. Stephanie hoped no one would notice she was late in the middle of all the confusion. But, as usual, her father seemed to have eyes in the back of his head.

"Five minutes past schedule, Steph," he said with a disappointed sigh. "*And* you forgot to call me at work and tell me you went to a friend's

8

house after school. I was worried about you all afternoon."

Stephanie frowned at her father's back. "But I told you this morning—I had to go to Allie's after school today."

"I know you did," Danny answered as he turned away from the stove. "But I still like you to call when you get where you're going. Then I know you're safe. And you also forgot to tell me exactly when you'd be getting home tonight. I've had to keep dinner warm for a full five minutes!"

Michelle sat down at the table and wrinkled her nose. "What *is* dinner, anyway?" she asked.

"It's that big meal at the end of the day," Joey joked. Everyone groaned.

Danny smiled and carried a big serving dish over to the table. "Dinner," he said, "is something I've invented myself. It's made out of rice, beans, cheese, spices, and beef. I'm thinking of calling it Mexican Taco Rice Surprise."

"I hope it's not *too* surprising," Joey remarked as he sat down next to Michelle.

"I hope it doesn't taste like a burnt rubber boot," said D.J., "like the last new dish you invented!"

"Very funny," Danny replied. "But I left the boot out of this recipe."

Everyone laughed except Stephanie. She was barely listening to the conversation. Instead, she was wondering when she should talk to her father about the big party Saturday night. And worrying about what he would say.

Danny took his place at the head of the table. "Anyone else who makes a joke about my cooking gets to clean up the entire kitchen tonight!" He opened his napkin and put it on his lap. "And now I want to answer the question I know you're all about to ask. Which is: Why are we having a *Mexican* dish on this particular night?"

"All right," Stephanie said. "I'll bite. Why are we having a Mexican dish on this particular night?"

"Glad you asked," Danny said with a laugh. "We're having a Mexican dish because I really miss being alone with my own little family sometimes. D.J.'s always off on a date or studying in the library. Stephanie's either on the phone or off doing something with a friend. And Michelle is either watching TV or out with Cassie."

Joey looked confused. "I feel your pain, Danny," he said. "But what does that have to do with Mexico?"

Danny smiled. "I figure, the only way to have my daughters all to myself is to get them away from all this. No friends, no telephones, no TV."

"Like, in Mexico?" D.J. asked. She looked as bewildered as Stephanie felt.

"Exactly!" Danny beamed. "Like somewhere in the middle of the desert. Somewhere we could all be together, with no interruptions." He scooped some Mexican Taco Rice Surprise onto his plate and took a taste. "Yum! This isn't bad at all. Pass your plates up to me, everybody, so we can dig in."

Stephanie stared at her father. Had it finally happened? Had her dad finally, totally flipped out?

"Let me get this straight," she said. "You want us to pretend we're in Mexico?"

"And we can't use the telephone or watch TV?" D.J. asked.

"Dad," Stephanie protested, "that is totally unfair!"

"I'm sure I shouldn't get involved, Danny,"

11

Joey said. "But I'm afraid I have to agree with the girls on this one."

Soon everybody at the table was talking at once, arguing with Danny about his crazy idea. Even Nicky and Alex got in on the act, shouting and banging their silverware on the table. Finally Danny waved his hands for silence.

"No, no, NO!" he shouted. "You've all got it wrong. I don't want us to *pretend* we're in Mexico. I want us to *go* to Mexico! Well, to New Mexico, actually." He reached into his pocket and pulled out a long envelope. "I already have the plane tickets. We leave on Saturday morning and stay for your whole spring break next week. Isn't it fantastic?"

"Fantastically *terrible!*" D.J. wailed. "I already have plans for spring break."

"Me, too," said Michelle. "I'm going Roller-blading!"

For a long moment Stephanie was too stunned to speak. At last she found her voice. "But, Dad," she cried, "Darcy and Allie and I are giving a party Saturday night. We already invited all the kids."

Danny frowned at her. "This is the first I've

heard about any party, Steph. How could you possibly be giving a party without my knowing about it?"

Stephanie's face turned red. "Um, I was going to ask you . . . that is, tonight, I was planning to—"

Danny interrupted her. "Well, all that is water under the bridge now. These are nonrefundable plane tickets. I was really lucky to find a replacement host for *Wake Up, San Francisco* for next week." He looked crushed. "I thought you'd all be pleased about this trip. Excited, even."

D.J. dropped her fork onto her plate. "Excited?" she repeated. "Now I have to break a date with Chad Greene! He's only the cutest boy in my class. He'll probably never ask me out again."

"I'm sorry you feel that way, girls." Danny frowned. "The Lazy O Dude Ranch sounds terrific—horses, hiking, cookouts, and fresh desert air. The perfect place to spend some quality time together."

"But, Dad—" Stephanie began to say.

"That's final," Danny said firmly.

Stephanie looked at her father and shook her head. *Terrific,* she thought as she lifted her fork. *So much for the party of the decade! Instead of dancing with the boy of my dreams, I get to spend spring break hanging with my dad and a bunch of smelly old cowboys!*

CHAPTER
2

◆ ◂ ◗ ◆

Nine o'clock in the morning and the New Mexico sun was already burning hot. Stephanie pulled her pale green T-shirt away from her body. It was soaked with sweat.

She hung her arms over the splintery top rail of the corral. *I can't believe this is Dad's idea of a good time,* she thought. *Five days at a boring pit like the Lazy O Dude Ranch!*

As she watched, three real-life cowboys on horseback galloped in front of her, chasing down a calf. The big, burly one in the red-checkered shirt was named Luke. He'd shown

15

the Tanners around the ranch yesterday when they arrived.

"Ya-hoo!" he yelled as he thundered by. His horse's hooves created a cloud of dust that blew into Stephanie's face. She coughed and turned away in time to see her father hurrying toward her.

"Stephanie?" he called. "Are you wearing sunscreen? This sun is really hot." He pulled a tube out of his backpack. "For your nose and mouth," he said. "They could burn to a crisp if you aren't careful."

So why'd you make us come out here if the sun's so dangerous? Stephanie felt like asking.

Stephanie blinked as she realized her father was smearing some thick, white gook onto the tip of her nose.

"Ugh! Dad, stop it! What is that stuff anyway?"

"Zinc oxide," Danny explained. "It'll protect your nose from the sun."

"And make me look like a clown!" Stephanie complained. She tried rubbing the lotion off her nose, but then she stopped and shrugged. What difference did it make, anyway? she asked herself. Who cared what she looked like in this place—there was no one there to see her, except calves and old cowboys like Luke.

It was only their first morning at the ranch, and Stephanie was already bored. There didn't seem to be any kids her own age around. The one bright spot was that Stephanie got to share her cabin with D.J. instead of Michelle. For once, her little sister wouldn't be underfoot all the time.

Of course, it had worked out that way because her dad didn't think Stephanie was old enough to take care of Michelle in a separate cabin. But Stephanie liked to think that she and D.J. were sharing because they were the oldest.

"Here's the schedule for the day," Danny said. "I've signed us up for everything. First, we're going riding. Then maybe we'll hike, or go swimming, or do arts and crafts. We can decide later. They even have Native American dancing here. Doesn't that sound fantastic?"

Fantastic, Stephanie thought bitterly. *I could be home dancing with Brandon Fallow tonight—if I hadn't been dragged to this place!*

Her father glanced at his watch. "Wow—I'm

late! I've got to get to the barn. I want to check out the horses they've picked for us to ride today. I want to be sure they choose extra-gentle horses for you girls." He hurried toward the barn.

D.J. and Michelle walked up. Michelle was dressed like a Native American, with a feather headdress that stretched to her heels, a turquoise necklace, and beaded leather moccasins. She had stripes of white and black paint on her forehead and cheeks.

"Hey," Michelle said when she saw Stephanie's white nose and lips, "are you taking Native American dance lessons, too?"

"No," Stephanie answered.

"So why is your face painted like mine?"

D.J. laughed. "It's not face painting, Michelle. It's zinc oxide, to keep from getting sunburned. Great look, Steph!"

Stephanie rolled her eyes. "It wasn't my idea," she said.

Michelle started rubbing at her face. "I'd better go wash this stuff off now," she said. "I have to go try out for the ranch play. They're having a show on our last day here."

D.J. smiled at Michelle. "I'm sure you'll get a part, Michelle," she said. "You were always a good actress in your school plays. But you won't have time to try out for the play right now. Dad signed us up for the trail ride, remember?"

"Yippeeyioh-kiyay!" Michelle shouted. "I get to ride on a real cowboy trail!"

"At least somebody around here's having a good time," Stephanie grumbled.

"Oh, come on, Steph," D.J. told her. "You might as well make the best of it. You know, I didn't want to come on this trip, either, but . . ."

D.J. suddenly stopped talking. The big, burly cowboy named Luke was coming toward them, leading several horses out of the stable. And next to Luke was a new cowboy, wearing faded jeans and a soft gray shirt. The new cowboy was young, tall, and really cute. Stephanie saw D.J.'s eyes get about three times bigger as she stared at him.

"This here's Joe," Luke told them, nodding at the young cowboy. "He'll help you saddle up."

Just then, Danny hurried up behind the cowboys. "Remember what I told you. I want gentle, well-mannered horses for these girls and—"

19

Luke cut him off. "Don't you worry. Joe here'll take good care of your gals." With a wink at Stephanie and her sisters, Luke led Danny away. "And I've got just the mount for you."

Stephanie looked at the horses. "Which one's mine?"

No one answered. She turned around and saw that D.J. and the cowboy named Joe were staring at each other so hard they hadn't even heard her! *Terrific,* she thought. *D.J. finds a boyfriend the first day we're here! And I'm stuck hanging around with Dad and Michelle!*

"Ex-*cuse* me!" she said loudly. "Which horse is mine?"

Absently Joe handed Stephanie a set of reins. They were attached to a horse with a sleek brown coat, a long white tail, and a silky white mane. Each of his legs was white up to the knee, almost as if he were wearing knee-highs. In spite of her bad mood, Stephanie thought he was beautiful.

"What's his name?" she asked.

"His . . . huh?" Joe turned away from D.J. and looked at her as if he'd never seen her before. "Did you say something?"

"What's my horse's name?"

"Oh, that's Blaze. And yours is Brownie, little girl," he told Michelle. He picked Michelle up and practically dumped her on the back of a small, dark brown pony. Then he went back to staring at D.J.

Stephanie sighed. She stroked her horse's velvety nose and whispered, "I think we're on our own here, Blaze." She wondered if she should wait for Joe or mount the horse alone. A quick glance told her that the cowboy had other things on his mind—like D.J.

"It's just you and me, boy," Stephanie told the horse. She put one foot in the stirrup and threw her other leg over the saddle. Blaze whinnied and lurched backward. For a moment Stephanie was thrown off balance. Then Blaze calmed down, and she got seated.

Good thing I took all those riding lessons at home, Stephanie thought.

"Time to move out!" Luke called from the front of the line. He turned his horse and trotted back to Stephanie. "Think you can handle Blaze?" he asked.

"Well, I have taken some riding lessons," Stephanie told him.

"Blaze has spirit," Luke said. "He's a good horse—try him out!"

"Okay." Stephanie shrugged. "Giddyup!" she said, digging her heels into Blaze's sides.

Blaze promptly bucked. His head went down, and his hind legs flew up in the air. Stephanie grabbed the saddle horn and held on for her life. Blaze snorted. Then his back legs hit the ground with a jarring thud.

D.J. pulled her black-and-white horse up to Stephanie. "Good grief!" she cried. "Don't be such a show-off."

"I'm not trying to show off!" Stephanie grasped Blaze tightly with her knees. He snorted again, but immediately settled down.

Stephanie glanced around quickly. *I hope Dad didn't see me!* she thought. If he had, he'd probably make her trade Blaze in for a fat old cow. Or worse yet, maybe he'd try to get her to share a horse with him!

She turned to look for her father. He was riding at the far back of the line. "What kind of horse is Dad riding, anyway?" Stephanie asked D.J. They both gazed at the long-eared, squat animal.

"I think it's a mule." D.J. giggled. "I guess they ran out of horses." Her face became serious. "Steph, do you really think you can handle that horse?"

"I think so," Stephanie said. The others were already out on the trail. "Let's catch up," Stephanie told D.J.

D.J. reined her horse around and hurried onto the trail. Stephanie was just about to follow when she stopped short. She drew in a deep breath and leaned forward in her seat. *Yes!* she thought. *I was right!* To one side of her was a very interesting rider. A slim boy who looked about her own age! He had shiny, dark brown hair that curled over the back of his green-and-white checked shirt. But what did his face look like?

As if answering her question, the boy turned and looked her way. He had sparkling blue eyes and a wide, dimpled smile. "Good handling," he called, nodding at Blaze. Stephanie felt herself blush.

"Justin!" someone called. Stephanie saw a woman riding up to the boy. She looked as if she might be his mother. "Better stay with me," the woman said. Justin nodded. Then he grinned at Stephanie. "Later!" he said before he rode off.

Stephanie was stunned. A boy her age! And not just any boy—a very cute, friendly boy! *Justin*. She said the name silently to herself. *Justin and Stephanie.* It sounded great! She could hardly believe her luck. Suddenly this vacation was really looking up!

CHAPTER
3

♦ ◂ ◂ ♦

Stephanie kicked Blaze again, but much more gently this time. She had to catch up with Justin! Blaze walked obediently forward, moving smoothly over the trail. Stephanie breathed a sigh of relief. Now that she had Blaze under control, she could catch up to Justin.

As smoothly as she could, Stephanie pulled around the three horses in front of her. Only four more horses to go, she told herself, and she'd be next to Justin again.

"Good Blaze," she said, stroking the horse's thick mane. "We're almost there."

Luke led the horses into a grassy meadow dotted with purple wildflowers.

This is so beautiful and romantic, Stephanie thought. *It's the perfect place to meet someone like Justin.*

It was time to make her move. She gave Blaze a firm kick in the sides—not too hard, not too gentle. But at the same instant a bee flew into Blaze's face!

With a wild whinny Blaze shot forward, yanking the reins out of Stephanie's hands.

"Whoa!" Stephanie shouted. "Nice horse! Stop!"

Blaze hurtled toward a huge tree stump. *He's going to jump it!* Stephanie thought frantically. *What should I do?* She'd never jumped a horse before! Sure, she'd had riding lessons, like she'd told Luke. But what she hadn't told him was that her lessons were mostly walking a tame, lazy horse around Golden Gate Park. She'd never ridden a bucking, jumping bronco before!

Blaze lifted his front legs and launched them over the stump. Stephanie was thrown forward in the saddle. She gripped Blaze's mane, afraid to lean back. Before she could scream, they'd already landed on the other side of the stump. The jolt made her teeth rattle. Somehow, she managed to stay on.

"Whoa, boy, whoa, Blaze!" she yelled.

She could hear Luke shouting in the background. "Pull him up!" he called.

Stephanie caught the reins and tried to do what Luke said. Blaze ignored her completely.

Suddenly the river loomed up. Jagged rocks stuck out of the foaming current. Blaze plunged headlong into the icy-cold water. "Stop, Blaze!" Stephanie yelled.

Blaze stopped. As if nothing unusual had happened, he lowered his head and started to drink, slurping up water in huge gulps. Stephanie heaved a huge sigh of relief.

"Now I've got you," she said. She hauled back on the reins. But instead of turning for shore, Blaze flopped down into the river!

"Yikes!" With a loud splash Stephanie fell off his back. She was drenched! Luckily the water was only about two feet deep.

Stephanie brushed wet, stringy hair out of her eyes. As she did, a thick glob of mud and zinc oxide came off onto her fingers. She could just imagine what she looked like.

"Hey!" someone called to her from the nearby bank. "You okay? Need some help?"

She stared in the direction of the voice. She saw a slim figure on horseback. Justin! His hair was still neatly in place. His green-and-white checked shirt was as spotless as when they'd started on the trail ride. He grinned at her.

"Hi again," he said. "Let me help you up."

He slid off his horse, then reached out a hand and pulled her to her feet.

"Thanks," Stephanie said shyly. Up close she could see that Justin had sky-blue eyes with little flecks of gold in them. Then a thick drop of muddy water rolled out of her hair and down her nose. She blinked and rubbed her nose with a muddy hand.

"Are you all right out there?" Luke yelled from the bank.

"Yes!" Stephanie yelled back. *Except for wanting to die of embarrassment,* she added to herself.

"Way to go, Steph!" D.J. called from the bank. "Nothing like an afternoon swim!"

Luke snorted with laughter. "No harm done.

28

I guess old Blaze got himself nice and cool!" He slapped his leg with his hat. Most of the other riders had come up behind him. Some of them were laughing, too.

Stephanie felt her face turn bright red. *Red face, brown mud, and zinc oxide,* she thought miserably. *No wonder they're laughing!*

"By the way, my name's Justin," the boy said. "Justin Anderson."

"I'm Stephanie Tanner." Stephanie paused. "And I don't usually look like this."

"I hope not." Justin laughed. His eyes twinkled at her. It was almost worth falling into a cold, muddy river. *He's not only cute,* she thought, *he's helpful and thoughtful, too. Too bad he'll never look at me again!*

"Hee-haw! Hee-haw!"

Stephanie groaned. Her father was kicking his mule through the crowd of riders on the bank.

"Stephanie! Stephanie!" he called. "Are you all right?"

"Yes, Dad!" she called back.

"Are you sure? Does anything hurt?"

Stephanie's cheeks turned even redder. Why did her father always have to make such a big deal out of everything? "I'm okay," she muttered.

As quickly as she could, Stephanie clambered up out of the river and onto the bank. Her father slid down off his mule and rushed over to her. "Stephanie," he said, "what in the world were you doing? Who told you to ride so fast?"

Stephanie shot a sideways glance at Justin and blushed even harder. How could she possibly explain that she'd wanted to catch up to a boy she'd barely met?

"Your saddle's broke," Luke told her. He held up a torn leather strap.

"She can ride with me," Danny offered.

Stephanie rolled her eyes. *Perfect!* she thought. *Now I get to ride on a mule!*

But Luke was shaking his head. "Nope," he said. "The mule's too small for two. She'll have to ride back with him." He jerked a finger at Justin.

"Okay," said Justin. He smiled at Stephanie, and her heart thumped. Maybe this wouldn't turn out to be so bad after all!

Justin led his pretty, golden-colored horse over to her. He swung easily into the saddle. "Hop on the back," he told Stephanie. "Behind me. Jet Stream won't mind carrying two of us."

"Thanks." Stephanie put her foot into the stirrup. One of the cowhands got behind her to push her into the saddle. He pushed so hard, Stephanie almost fell off the other side of the horse. *Could this day get any worse?* she thought. Thankfully, Justin kept Jet Stream steady while she got settled in the saddle.

Danny rode out of the crowd of riders on his mule. "Stephanie," he said, "I'd really feel safer if you were riding with me."

Justin's mother appeared at his side. "I would, too, Justin," she said. She turned to Danny. "I'm his mother, Claire Anderson. And I agree with you."

Danny sighed with relief. "Nice to meet you, Claire," he said. "I'm Danny Tanner, Stephanie's father. And I think these kids had enough excitement for one morning."

"Dad, we're fine," Stephanie said. "You heard what Luke said. The mule's too small to hold two people."

"She's right, Mr. Tanner." Luke rode up next to them. "They'll do right fine on Jet Stream.

I don't know what got into Blaze back there. Something must have spooked him."

"Maybe so," Danny said, "but if we do any more riding this week, I want to be sure that Stephanie's on a much safer horse!"

Luke winked at Stephanie. "I'll tame Blaze down myself," he promised her dad.

"Well, okay," Danny finally agreed. He peered at Stephanie. "I think you need more zinc oxide on your nose."

Stephanie groaned. "I put on enough to last all week!"

"I have zinc oxide." Claire Anderson reached into her saddlebag and drew out a tube. She handed it to Justin.

"Let's get rolling, folks!" Luke swatted Danny's mule, and the riders headed out on the trail again.

Justin twisted around in the saddle. He handed Stephanie the tube of zinc oxide. "If you rub it really hard, it almost disappears," he told her.

"Thanks," Stephanie answered.

Justin grinned at her. "Looks like we have something in common," he said.

"What's that?" Stephanie asked.

"Parents," Justin joked. "Parents who worry a lot."

Stephanie felt about ten times better!

Justin flicked the reins, and Jet Stream started moving up the trail. "Uh ... how do I hold on?" Stephanie asked, grabbing at the back of the saddle.

"Put your arms around me," Justin told her.

Stephanie couldn't believe this was really happening. She was putting her arms around the cutest boy in the world. And he'd asked her to!

Justin spoke over his shoulder. "You can really ride," he said.

Stephanie couldn't believe her ears. "Do you think so?" she asked.

"Yeah. You looked really good going over that jump."

Jump? Oh, the stump! "Really?" If Justin had been impressed with the way she'd looked on Blaze, she was definitely keeping the horse all week. "Well, I have had some riding lessons," she said.

"I've been riding all my life," Justin said. "I take lessons in Boston, where I live."

"Boston? I'm from San Francisco." Stephanie's heart sank. They couldn't live any father away!

"Not exactly neighbors." Justin laughed, as if he'd read her mind. "But that's something else we have in common—we're both from big cities."

"Yeah!" Stephanie felt happier. "Thanks for your help in the river back there."

"No problem," Justin answered.

No problem! Happily Stephanie tightened her grip around Justin's waist.

It felt as if no time had passed before they were back at the ranch. All around them strange, weird-shaped orange rocks rose into the sky.

"Wow," Stephanie gasped. She had to admit, it was really spectacular. Suddenly she was really glad she had come on this vacation. She had never seen any place so dramatic and beautiful. And she was seeing it all with the coolest boy she'd ever met!

CHAPTER
4

◆ ◀ ◼ ◆

Stephanie rubbed her arm. Every muscle in her body ached—thanks to her wild horseback ride that morning. But Stephanie didn't mind. She'd do it all again if it meant she could spend more time with Justin. Of course, this time, she'd be sure to have dry hair and a cool outfit. The way she was dressed right now. She turned on the picnic bench, searching for Justin in the crowd.

"Stephanie, you're not listening to me!"

Michelle poked her in the arm. Stephanie almost dropped her paper plate. It was loaded full of spareribs, beans, and coleslaw. The guests at the dude ranch were being treated to their first evening cookout. A few feet away stood the chuck wagon, kind of an outdoor kitchen on wheels. In front of it a campfire burned briskly. The camp cook stood in front of the fire. Burgers, hot dogs, and ribs sizzled over the giant grill.

"Stephanie!" Michelle whined again.

Stephanie pretended she hadn't heard. The last thing she needed was to listen to one of her little sister's dumb stories. All she cared about right now was spotting Justin—and letting him see her in her new fringed cowboy vest, with a clean face and shiny hair.

But Michelle wouldn't give up. "Stephanie," she said again, "I'm trying to tell you, I got my part in the camp play!"

"That's nice," Stephanie answered. She craned her neck. Justin wasn't in the crowd of campers around the grill. She didn't see him, but she did see D.J., laughing and talking with Joe. She felt a little pang of jealousy. Where was Justin, anyway? What if he was avoiding Stephanie? Maybe he didn't want to see her after all.

"Dad said you could help me learn my lines. Okay?"

Stephanie barely heard her. "Lines?" she repeated. "Oh sure, Michelle. Anytime."

"It's a big part, Steph. I'm the lead—Annie Oakley. So I really have a lot of stuff to learn, and—"

"Hush, Michelle! I *said* I'd help you, all right?" Stephanie leaned forward on her seat and stared. *Yes!* she thought. *There he is!*

Justin had appeared in the front of the line by the grill. The cook was just serving him a juicy burger. Justin had changed into a forest-green sweatshirt and black jeans. He looked handsomer than ever.

Stephanie felt like jumping up and running over to him, but she made herself sit still. She didn't want to seem too pushy. *Please let him come sit with me,* she silently willed. She was sure that if Justin *didn't* come, it meant he'd just been being polite that afternoon. It meant he wasn't interested in her at all. And that she'd made a total fool of herself on the trail ride.

Anxiously she watched him pick out bread. Then he served himself salad from the buffet table next to the chuck wagon. Next, he paused—practically forever—in front of the dessert tray. Finally he chose a slab of pecan pie with whipped cream.

"Now!" Stephanie whispered. She laughed out loud, as if Michelle had said something adorable. At the same time she scooted over on the log seat, making room for another person.

Justin hesitated, looked around—and then walked to a different picnic table. He sat down next to his mother. Stephanie slumped in disappointment. *Well, at least he didn't find another girl,* she told herself.

But she didn't feel like eating anymore. She put her plate down on the ground and picked up a stick. Slowly she drew an upside-down heart in the dirt. Suddenly she felt terrible.

Danny had been talking to one of the other guests. Now he walked over and sat down next to her. "Eat up, Stephanie. You're going to need your strength. I signed us up for a cliff hike tomorrow. We're going to see some petroglyphs."

"What are petroglyphs?" Michelle wanted to know.

"Ancient Indian carvings," Danny explained. "They're over a thousand years old."

"Sounds boring," Michelle said.

"I agree." Stephanie nodded. "Who wants to see a bunch of old carvings anyway?"

Danny looked shocked. "I'm surprised at you kids. There's exciting stuff all around us here. That's what's so great about New Mexico. You're going to love this hike. And I'm going to love seeing petroglyphs with my whole family together," Danny said, smiling. "Me and my three little girls."

"Dad," Michelle said, "can we go get some pie?"

"Sure." Danny sighed. "Want a piece, Steph?"

"Whatever," Stephanie answered.

Michelle and Danny got to their feet and walked over to the dessert table. Stephanie picked up her stick again and drew another big heart in the ground. This time she drew a jagged line through the middle.

"Hi, Stephanie. Do you mind if I sit here?"

Stephanie looked up and swallowed hard. It was Justin! He was smiling down at her, holding his pie and soda. "Mind? N-no," she stammered. "Go ahead and sit."

"I would have come over before," Justin explained, "but I didn't recognize you without mud and zinc oxide on your face!"

Stephanie giggled. "I guess I did look pretty awful," she said.

"Oh, not so bad," Justin said. He glanced over at her. "Though you do look a lot better now." He looked down shyly. "Your hair is amazing. It keeps changing in the firelight."

"Changing?"

"Yes. It's a different color every time the fire changes. First it's a reddish yellow, then it's gold. It's kind of pretty."

Stephanie couldn't believe her ears. Justin had been watching her! He thought she had pretty hair. And she'd thought he didn't like her!

"What grade are you in?" Justin asked.

"Seventh," Stephanie said. "How about you?"

"I'm in eighth. I just turned fourteen."

Perfect! Stephanie thought. *Wait till I tell Darcy and Allie.* "I saw you sitting with your mom before," she said.

"Yes. She's raising me alone," Justin said. "And since we're here alone, I have to do a lot of stuff with her. It gets kind of hard sometimes."

Stephanie rolled her eyes. "Tell me about it."

Justin laughed. "She made me go on a hike with her after the trail ride. I didn't want to go—but it turned out pretty cool. She told me all about these weird desert plants, like those round green ones called tumbleweeds. And these short little pine trees called junipers. They look like something from a science fiction movie! I'm getting to like the desert, I guess."

Stephanie nodded. "I know what you mean. When we first got here, I thought it was just hot and boring. But the stuff we saw on the trail ride was really amazing." *Including you*, she added to herself.

"Wow! Talk about amazing—look at that sunset over there."

Stephanie looked where Justin was pointing. The sun was disappearing behind the flat-topped mesas. From behind the rocky hills, rays of pink and gold shot into the pale blue sky. It was even more amazing, because down in the valley where they were, darkness was falling fast.

"It's fantastic," Stephanie said. "This ranch is turning out to be a really cool place."

"You know what?" Justin said. "My mom made me sign up for that petroglyph hike tomorrow, and I was wondering—"

"Excuse me, young man," said a voice. "I believe that's my seat you're sitting in."

Stephanie's father was bearing down on them with three platefuls of pie. She bit her lip. Justin was just about to ask her for a real date!

Stephanie's cheeks flamed. "Dad, you remember Justin," she said pointedly. "He wanted to eat dessert with *me*."

Naturally Danny didn't take the hint. "Hi, Justin." He nodded politely. "Steph—I found a great stick for roasting marshmallows. I think we can even reach the fire from here."

"Dad, let's do the marshmallows a little later?" Stephanie emphasized the word *later*.

"Why later?" Danny asked. He stuck a marshmallow on one of the sticks. "The marshmallows are here, we're here, and there's the fire."

Justin got to his feet. "I guess I should go now," he said. "Stephanie, do you think you'll be going on that hike I was telling you about?"

Stephanie smiled. "You mean, to the petroglyphs? Well, I really think—" she began.

"She thinks they're boring," Danny broke in. "But it doesn't matter. I just heard about something else you'll love—a basket-weaving workshop! Sounds good, huh, Steph? Not like some boring old carvings." Danny looked proud of himself. "And the whole family can still do it together. You, me, Michelle, and D.J."

Stephanie's mouth fell open. She was so shocked she could barely speak. "But, uh, Dad . . . the carvings—"

"That's too bad," Justin said before Stephanie could finish. He started to walk away. "I guess I'll see you around some other time, Stephanie."

"Yeah, some other time," she said. Stephanie turned to her father. She *had* to say something! "Dad," she began, "you practically told Justin to leave!"

Her father frowned. "Wait a minute, Stephanie. Justin seems nice and I know you like boys. But this vacation is supposed to be about family time. You'll have plenty of time for schoolgirl crushes back home."

Stephanie couldn't believe it! Justin wasn't just another crush! She would have said so, too, but the look on her father's face warned her not to.

Instead, she sighed. "Goodbye, Justin—hello basket weaving," she muttered under her breath.

Stephanie sprawled over the bed in the cabin she shared with her older sister. "D.J.," she said, "what do you do when Dad drives you out of your mind?"

D.J. was lying on her own bed, writing a postcard. "Like when he makes you crazy, nuts, bonkers?" D.J. laughed. "He wouldn't be Dad if he didn't do that." She put down her pen and looked at Stephanie. "What's he done now?"

"The basket-weaving workshop! Justin practically asked me on a date, and instead, Dad interrupts and says I have to go basket weaving!" Stephanie groaned. "And there's nothing I can do about it."

"That's tough," D.J. agreed.

"Yeah. Justin wanted me to go on the petroglyph hike."

"And all of a sudden you're totally fascinated with petroglyphs?"

Stephanie giggled. "Totally," she agreed. "Now I'm dying to see them."

D.J. chewed on the end of her pen. "Hmmm,"

she said. "I don't blame you for being upset. Justin *is* pretty cute."

"D.J.! He's only in eighth grade. He's way too young for you."

"I didn't say I was interested in him," D.J. teased. "Just that he was cute."

Stephanie frowned. "But what am I going to do about tomorrow?"

D.J. sat back. "Dad's not such a big problem," she said.

"How can you say that? He's trying to ruin my life!"

"He's just being Dad, that's all. He just wants to spend time with you."

"But what can I *do* about it, D.J.? If I don't get to go on that hike tomorrow, I'll die!"

"Wow, Steph," D.J. said, "you should be in the camp play. You make it sound so dramatic."

"Come on, D.J. If this were about you, and you couldn't go for a hike with cowboy Joe, wouldn't you be upset, too?"

D.J. put down her postcard. "I guess you're right," she said slowly. "And Joe said he'd give me rope-throwing lessons tomorrow. So I may have a problem with Dad myself." She thought for a minute. "You know," she went on, "I've learned that the best way to handle Dad is to be honest with him. First thing tomorrow, go to Dad and explain that you really like this boy, Justin, and—"

"You have to be kidding!" Stephanie cried. "I can't tell him that! Oh, sure, he thinks it's okay for you to like a boy. You're older—you're almost finished with high school. But Dad still thinks I'm a little baby! If I tell him I really like someone, he'll lock me in the barn and feed the key to the cows!"

Stephanie flopped down on her bunk and pulled her pillow over her head. *Why me?* she asked herself again and again. *Why did I get the most overprotective father in the whole wide world?*

CHAPTER
5

◆ ◀ ◗ ◆

As soon as breakfast was over, Stephanie ran to the ranch house. She wanted to buy postcards to send to Darcy and Allie. She hadn't forgotten her friends completely—and she had so much to tell them!

Also, last night was their big boy-girl party. Stephanie wished she could have called them last night to ask about it, but Danny had given D.J. an especially long lecture on his vacation rules. Absolutely no phone calls. "Not for any reason," he'd said, "except an emergency."

Stephanie had just picked up a postcard show-

47

ing an incredibly complicated petroglyph when her father walked into the ranch house. All at once, she had an idea.

"Dad, look at this," she said. "Isn't this petro-glyph amazing? It makes me really want to go on that hike today."

Danny looked surprised. "I thought you weren't interested in a bunch of boring old carvings."

"Did I say that? Well, this picture shows just how wrong I was. Petroglyphs are totally fascinating."

"Well," Danny said slowly, "if you feel that way . . ."

"And," Stephanie went on, "the hike would be a great opportunity for you and me and Michelle to spend some time together—since D.J.'s not going to basket weaving anyway."

"She's not?" Danny asked.

"No. She said something about rope-throwing lessons."

Danny's face fell. "Well, Michelle's not going, either. She has to stay and practice her part in the camp play."

"Then, it's perfect!" Stephanie said. "I mean,

it's a perfect chance for you and me to be together."

Danny rubbed his chin with his fingers. "Hmmm. I am glad you're interested in the petroglyphs. And it is a good chance to spend time together. So, great! This will be fun."

Stephanie threw her arms around her father's neck. *I'm going on the hike!* she thought excitedly. Of course, it wasn't the same as going with Justin *alone*, but it was better than nothing!

"Oh, it will be fun, Dad!" Stephanie cried. "I know it will! Thank you."

Danny hugged Stephanie back. "Come on now," he said. "We'd better hurry if we're going. Everyone has to saddle up soon."

"Saddle up? Why?" Stephanie asked.

"The petroglyphs are pretty far away. We have to ride most of the way to get close to the hiking trail." He sighed. "I suppose you'll have to ride Blaze again. I hope Luke really did tame that horse."

"I'm sure he did." Stephanie quickly paid for her postcards and put them in her back pocket. "I'm ready, Dad," she said.

When they got outside, they saw D.J. was already in the corral. She was holding a lariat, and Joe was standing right beside her.

"So that's how you toss it," Joe was saying.

"Like this?" D.J. gripped the rope and threw it. It flew toward a couple of brown-and-white calves at the far end of the corral. The rope fell, nowhere near the calves.

"Close, darlin'. Let me show you again." Joe reached around her from the back and positioned her hands. D.J. smiled.

Stephanie grinned. *Suddenly she just has to learn about calf-roping!* she thought.

"Uh, D.J.," Danny called. "Don't stand so close to Joe. You need room to swing." Danny looked worried. "I hope we do something together, later," Danny added.

"Sure! I'll see you at dinner," D.J. answered. "Maybe we can do something later tonight."

"Okay, sweetheart. Be sure to keep an eye on Michelle from time to time. All the actors are behind the ranch house." He turned to Stephanie. "Come on, Steph. Let's go pick out our horses."

At that moment Justin rode up on Jet Stream, his cream-colored palomino. "Stephanie," he said. "Did you change your mind? Are you coming on the hike after all?"

"Um, yes," Stephanie said. "I am."

"Great! The horses are all saddled up." He flashed a smile at her. "Want a lift over to the stable?"

"Yes," Stephanie said. "Okay, Dad?" Before Danny could answer, Justin had reached down to help her swing into the saddle behind him. She put her arms around his waist. "See you in a minute, Dad," she said as they rode off.

When they got to the stable, Stephanie saw that Luke was holding Blaze for her. *Oh, no,* she thought. She felt a flutter of panic in her stomach. Would Blaze run away with her again? Would he crash through the trees, plunge across the river, and buck her into those very hard-looking orange rocks in the desert? Even just dumping her in the river again would be terrible.

But then she remembered—Justin had been really impressed with the way she'd handled Blaze. Maybe she'd impress him all over again today.

She slid off Jet Stream's side. "Here you go," Luke said, handing her Blaze's reins. Luke's cheek was bulging with a gigantic tobacco chaw. "No funny business today," he said to the horse.

Stephanie took the reins and stood there for a second. *Just get on!* she ordered herself. She swung her leg up over the horse and sank into the saddle.

"You look great on him," Justin told her. His eyes were shining with admiration.

"Thanks." Blaze stood quietly. Stephanie patted him gently. "Good horse," she murmured. She waited a minute to make sure he was really calm. All at once she heard a loud "Hee haw!"

Her father was at the far end of the corral, mounting the mule he'd ridden yesterday. Stephanie felt a pang of guilt for riding off with Justin. Maybe she shouldn't have, but her dad didn't understand that Justin was *more* than just another crush.

Justin pulled Jet Stream over beside her, and they rode out of camp together. The sky was an incredible pale turquoise. In the strong sun the desert sand shone a brilliant white.

"Are you going to do more stunt riding today?" Justin asked her with a laugh.

"I sure hope not." Stephanie eyed Blaze

warily. So far he was just plodding along like the other horses. She hoped he would stay that way.

They were soon into the open desert. "My mother made me bring her book about desert plants," Justin said. He pointed to it, stuck into his shirt pocket.

"I thought she wanted to come with you," Stephanie said curiously.

"She did," Justin said. "But she was so sore from yesterday's ride she had to sleep in this morning. She told me to go ahead and enjoy myself. That *never* happens."

"I wish it would happen to me," Stephanie muttered.

"Hey, look—there's a tumbleweed over there." Justin pointed. "Usually, they grow where the land is disturbed. Like, by animals grazing or construction or something."

"I guess the ranch is pretty disturbing," Stephanie joked.

Justin laughed at her joke. He told her some more stuff from the plant book. Stephanie was surprised to find it pretty interesting.

After fifteen minutes they had reached the orange cliffs Stephanie had seen from the ranch.

They rode up a steep path, over loose rocks. Stephanie had to drop Blaze back behind Justin and Jet Stream to ride single file. A while later, the path leveled off and widened again.

"Look at those plants—they're growing right out of the cliffs!" she called to Justin. Blaze yanked at the reins, trying to reach a tuft of grass growing out of a crack.

"Blaze! It's not lunchtime!" Stephanie pulled back hard on the reins.

Blaze yanked the reins right through her hands. He tossed his head—and bucked. Stephanie's stomach lurched as they went airborne. *Not again!* she thought. *Oh, no!*

She almost fell off as they hit the ground. She felt a burst of fear. She swallowed hard, trying to get control of herself. She tried to get her balance, but Blaze bucked again. The ground zoomed by at a dizzying angle. Stephanie saw Luke ride up next to them, trying to grab Blaze's reins.

"He's hopping like a jackrabbit!" Luke said.

Suddenly the fear disappeared. Now Stephanie was angry. Blaze was making her look like an idiot, bouncing her around like this! She grabbed up the reins and pulled back on them hard.

Blaze snorted in surprise and dropped to the ground. The next second he was walking like a normal horse!

"Now settle down," Stephanie told him sternly. "Or you'll get more of that!"

"Thatta girl!" Luke cheered. "Show him who's boss."

Justin cantered over to her. His blue eyes were full of admiration. "What a ride! You're really amazing."

"Thanks." *That was quite a ride*, Stephanie thought. She was pretty pleased with herself. After all, Blaze weighed about twelve hundred pounds, and she had made him mind. Not bad. She was really starting to like this dude ranch stuff.

Luke looked around and yelled, "Okay, everybody! Tie the horses here. We'll hike now—the path's getting too rocky to ride."

"I think I just had a rocky ride!" Stephanie told Justin. She was glad to slide out of the saddle and tie Blaze to a stunted tree. As she did, she suddenly remembered her father. *If he saw me showing off for Justin,* she worried, *he'll make me ride back to the ranch on his mule!*

Luckily, her father turned out to be far ahead of her, hurrying after the cowboys. He'd missed the entire fight with Blaze. *What amazing luck!* Stephanie thought. *Everything is going right!*

The cowboys herded everyone over to one of the cliffs. Stephanie's father turned and waved her over to him. As Stephanie got closer, she saw what her dad was looking at. Somebody had chiseled a bird right into the smooth face of the black rock. It wasn't a very realistic carving, like a photograph, but the artist had managed to capture the feeling you got, watching a bird fly free.

"This petroglyph is a parrot," Luke told the group. "It's about a thousand years old. Thing is, there weren't any parrots native to New Mexico a thousand years ago. So whoever drew this bird must have seen a parrot in Old Mexico, south of the border. That's hundreds of miles from here."

"This is exciting stuff, isn't it?" Danny whispered in Stephanie's ear.

Stephanie nodded. To her surprise, she did find the story about the parrot interesting.

Luke paused to spit tobacco at a rock. "The next thing we'll see is the old pueblo," he said. "A pueblo is a series of ancient cave dwellings. Several tribes have lived there over the past thousand or so years. A couple of centuries ago Spanish soldiers conquered the last tribe of pueblo Indians and moved out.

"But, to this day, some people believe the pueblo is enchanted. The story is, one of the Spanish soldiers fell in love with an Indian princess. And she fell in love with him. The tribe wasn't too fond of the Spanish, of course. So her people wouldn't give her up. Instead, they killed the Indian princess. Meanwhile, the soldier was killed by the Spanish. Anything to keep those lovers apart. Some folks say their ghosts haunt the caves, looking for each other." Luke spat some tobacco at a rock. "Course, I think it's a load of bunk."

Stephanie clasped her hands together. *I don't think it's a load of bunk.* She thought the story of the two doomed lovers was terribly sad—and very romantic. She glanced sideways at Justin, to see what he was thinking. But where was Justin?

Stephanie had to step aside then, to let someone else get a closer look at the petroglyph. As she did, she spotted Justin up between two towering rocks. He tilted his head toward a small path and motioned for her to join him.

Stephanie hesitated. She thought back to all the warnings her father had given her at the beginning of this trip. "Never wander off in strange surroundings" had been at the top of his list.

But we're not really wandering off, Stephanie told herself. *And I won't really be by myself. I'll be with Justin!*

She shot a glance back at her father. Danny was listening hard to Luke's lecture. As quietly as she could, Stephanie followed Justin away from the group. A minute later she stepped between the two big rocks. Justin had found a steep path on the other side that led away from the group below.

"Let's go exploring," Justin said. Together, they hurried up the path. There were all sorts of fascinating rocks, and lots of strange plants. Justin looked them all up in his plant book. It was great, being with him. Together, they wandered from rock to rock, going farther and farther up the trail. At one point Justin was far ahead of her.

"Look at this!" he called. He was standing on an orange-and-tan rock that was shaped like a wishbone. It was truly amazing. Stephanie ran to join him.

"New Mexico used to be underwater, millions of years ago," Justin told her. "About when the earth's polar icecaps melted."

"Speaking of ice, I'm really thirsty," Stephanie said. She'd forgotten both of her canteens today. Maybe her father was right to check up on her every single morning.

"No problem. There's a little spring over here," Justin said, pointing behind some rocks. Stephanie followed him and gasped out loud. A lovely miniature waterfall was running right out of a crack in the rock.

Justin hesitated. "I'm not sure if it's safe to drink this water," he said.

"We'd better not," Stephanie agreed. "Let's find the group again. I can get a drink from somebody's canteen."

"Good idea," Justin said. "Besides, we should get back before they notice we're gone."

But when they came back around the two big rocks, everyone else had disappeared.

"Uh-oh," Stephanie said. "This is not good. How long were we gone, anyway?"

"Almost half an hour," Justin told her.

Stephanie couldn't believe it. "That long? My dad will be frantic."

"Maybe we can catch up if we run." Justin looked back down the trail. "Come on, let's go." He took Stephanie's hand.

Stephanie's heart thumped. She couldn't believe it! Justin was holding her hand!

They flew over the trail. It was hard going, in the hot sun. Finally they rounded a bend—and there was the group! Stephanie realized everyone had seen her holding hands with Justin. But the thought didn't make her happy. It just made her worried—what would her father say? Then she spotted him—and Stephanie knew they were in big trouble.

"Stephanie! We've been looking everywhere for you!" Danny cried. His voice was tight with worry and anger. "How could you go off alone like that? Especially without telling any of the grownups where you'd be!"

Stephanie wanted to hide under a rock. "I'm sorry, Dad," she muttered.

"Well, you should be, young lady. We're going to have a long talk about this."

Stephanie was embarrassed and ashamed. But she was also angry. Did her father always have to scold her in front of other people?

"Okay!" Luke yelled then. "We found our missing cowpokes. But that's it for the hike. We don't have time now to visit the Indian pueblo— it's another half mile up the trail. Instead, let's head for the swimming hole."

Danny's forehead creased. "I'm sticking by you for the rest of the trip," he told her. At least he had lowered his voice. "Did you really come along to look at petroglyphs?" he asked. "Or was that line just an excuse to see Justin?"

Stephanie's face turned red. "Dad, do we have to talk about this now?"

"No, I guess not. But we'll certainly talk about it later!"

The group arrived at the swimming hole. It was a deep-set pool of water, surrounded by towering orange cliffs. The water shimmered blue, reflecting the sky.

Luckily Stephanie had remembered to put on her bathing suit under her clothes. She pulled off her shirt and edged away from her father. Just then she saw Justin diving into the water. He had on a red-and-white surfer bathing suit. Stephanie wished she'd brought something cooler than her plain old black tank suit.

She stepped into the water and started moving in Justin's direction. He saw her and swam over to her. "Hi," he said.

"Hi."

A dark, wet shape rose up between them. It was Danny. "Hi," he said. "Isn't this water refreshing? Stephanie, be sure you don't swim out too deep. And be careful about stepping on sharp or slippery rocks." He turned to Justin. "Once, when she was a little girl, she slipped on a rock in deep water and panicked. I had to swim out and save her."

Stephanie wanted to scream. "Dad, I was only six years old!"

"Well, six years old or twelve years old, you still have to be careful."

It was time for a change of subject. "I'm hungry," she announced. "I think I'll go eat some lunch."

"Me, too," Justin said.

Stephanie waited for her father to say, "Me, three." But, to her surprise, he said he wanted to swim for a few more minutes. "Be sure to eat something high energy, Steph," he said. "I packed some low-fat cheese and crackers in my backpack." He dived back under the water.

"Okay," Stephanie called to him. She turned to Justin. "I'm really sorry about my dad. He's unbelievable sometimes."

"So's my mom," Justin admitted. "And there's only one of me. Your dad must go crazy trying to keep up with three kids."

"Well, he has some help at home," Stephanie said. She and Justin dried themselves off. Then they took out their food and sat down on a warm rock. As they ate, Stephanie told him all about her big family. About Uncle Jesse and Aunt Becky, Nicky and Alex, and Joey and even Comet, the dog. As she talked, Justin really listened, smiling and nodding his head and asking questions in all the right places.

"Enough of this healthy food," he said after a few minutes. "It's time for the good stuff." He reached into his backpack and pulled out two bags of M&M's. "My favorite! One for you and one for me! Usually I don't share this, but, in your case, I'll bend the rules."

Stephanie's heart skipped a beat. "Those are my favorite, too," she said. "That's something else we have in common." *And I'll bet there's a lot more, too.*

She looked up at the blue sky and sighed happily. The sky was as clear and bright as her mood.

"I wanted to ask you something," Justin said then.

Justin looked so serious, Stephanie wondered what was on his mind. "Sure," she said. "What?"

"Do you have any plans for tomorrow afternoon?"

Stephanie's heart began to race. *Is he asking me on a date?* she thought. *Can this really be happening?*

"No," she said, trying to keep her voice calm, "I don't have any plans."

"Well, there's a covered-wagon ride tomorrow. Luke said I could sit on the wagonboard and help drive the team. I was wondering, um . . . if you'd . . ." His voice trailed away.

"Boy, I'd really like to help with the horses," she said helpfully.

"Yeah!" Justin grinned. "You are good with horses. So, would you sit up front with me on the wagon?"

Would I? "I'd love to," Stephanie said. Somehow, she kept from jumping up and down. *Yes!* she cried to herself. *This is a real date! My first real date! Darcy and Allie—you'll never believe this!* Stephanie was so excited she could hardly stand it! The only problem was, would her father ever let her go?

CHAPTER
6

♦ ◀ ◗ ♦

Stephanie squirmed on the picnic bench. Her whole family was at dinner that night, and Stephanie was bursting to tell someone about her first real date. But D.J. was deep in conversation with Joe at one end of the picnic table. No way could Stephanie get her attention. Michelle was too little to understand how important this was. And, as for her father . . . well, Stephanie didn't want to talk to him at all. She was sure he'd think she was too young to go on a date—especially after today's disaster on the petroglyphs hike.

Her father finished eating and crumpled his paper plate. "Tomorrow's wagon ride sounds really exciting," Danny said. "At last we can all go together, as a family." He tossed his plate into a trash can. "Two points!" he exclaimed. Then he looked around. "Don't I get two points for bringing us to this ranch? Aren't we having a good time?"

Stephanie smiled at him. "Yeah, Dad," she said sincerely. "Couldn't be better. And the wagon ride sounds *really* exciting." *More than you know!* she added to herself.

She got up from the table. "In fact, I've got to write Allie and Darcy all about it. I'll see you all later."

Danny followed her. "Stephanie," he began, "about the hike this afternoon—"

"Dad," Stephanie broke in, "I really didn't mean to worry you so much—or to ruin the hike for all the other guests."

Danny ruffled her hair. "I know you didn't, honey," he said. "And, frankly, that's what I'm worried about. Just because a boy asked you, you wandered off without thinking. And without telling me. Can't you see what poor judgment that was?"

Stephanie felt genuinely guilty. "You're right, Dad. I'm really sorry."

"I can see that you are, sweetheart. I've been trying to think of the right way to punish you—maybe I should ground you? Make you miss the wagon ride tomorrow . . . ?"

"Dad! Not that!"

Danny put his arm around her. "Okay, not that," he agreed. "I think you truly regret what you did. So we'll forget about it. Just be sure you don't do something that silly again!"

"I won't, Dad. I promise."

Danny gave her a hug. "Okay. Now go write those postcards."

Stephanie walked to her cabin with a big grin on her face. She couldn't believe it—her father had forgiven her. She could go on her first date! Now, if only she could tell him the truth about the wagon ride.

As soon as she got inside the cabin, her heart began to pound with nervousness. *What will I talk about with Justin?* she asked herself. Were things different on a date? What should she wear? Should she dress up, or go casual? And what about makeup? Would her father let her wear mascara and lipstick—on a wagon ride?

Her head pounded with questions. She really needed to get some advice from D.J. But her sister was off with Joe somewhere. If only she could talk with Darcy and Ally. But they were in San Francisco, a thousand miles away.

Stephanie looked at the phone on the nightstand. Danny had told D.J. the cabin rules—absolutely no long-distance phone calls. But Danny hadn't told *her* that, Stephanie reasoned.

The phone sat silently on the table. Stephanie stared at it a few seconds longer. Then she grabbed it up and punched in Allie's number. One ring later Allie picked up.

"Hey, Allie!" Stephanie said.

"Stephanie!" Allie squealed. "Oh, I'm so glad you called! Wait—Darcy's here right now. I'll tell her to get on the extension."

Stephanie settled herself comfortably on the bed, plumping up the pillow. It felt so good to hear Allie's voice.

"Is that really you?" Darcy was on the line.

"You guys sound so close—like you're in the cabin next door," Stephanie said, kicking off her cowboy boots and propping her feet up against the wall. "I wish you were!"

"What's it like out there?" Darcy asked. "Are there cowboys and cows and ghost towns everywhere?"

"Well, D.J.'s made friends with a cowboy," said Stephanie. "And a few cows, too! I think she's roped them both. And there really is a ghost town. An Indian pueblo, right outside the ranch. They say the spirits of two doomed lovers wander around it at night."

"Cool," said Allie.

Neither of them sounds mad about the party, Stephanie thought. "Well . . . how did things go on Saturday night?" she asked.

"Oh, Steph, it was horrible!" Allie wailed. "You won't believe what happened!"

Stephanie felt bad about ditching her friends all over again. "Try me," she said.

"When we found out you weren't coming, we sort of chickened out." Darcy took over the story. "I mean, we still had it, but . . . we ended up inviting Flamingoes, just to make sure it wasn't a total flop."

"You didn't!" How could Darcy and Allie invite those social snobs? "What did they do?" Stephanie asked.

"What *didn't* they do!" Allie said gloomily. "They stole our boyfriends! Or, I mean, the guys we *wanted* for our boyfriends. Diana Rink spent the whole party talking to Jason. He was supposed to be *mine*. Then Jenni Morris fed Dylan chips for hours, so he couldn't have talked to anybody even if he wanted to!"

"Dylan certainly didn't talk to me," Darcy chimed in. "So Allie and I talked to each other the whole time."

"Boy, that's really bad. But wait till you hear what happened to me," Stephanie said. "I met this incredible—"

"No, no, you have to listen to the rest of this," Allie interrupted. "Stealing our guys wasn't even the worst thing the Flamingoes did. Diana and Jenni invited us out with Jason and Dylan on a group date."

"With four girls and two boys? What kind of date is *that?*" Stephanie asked. She wished Darcy and Allie would finish the story of the party so that she could tell them about her *real* date!

"We're going bowling, all six of us," Darcy said.

"Why?" Stephanie asked. Darcy and Allie had flipped while she was away. "You'll just be third wheels. Or fifth and sixth wheels, I guess."

"We have some self-esteem, Stephanie," Darcy said. "We thought if we hung around with Jason and Dylan enough, they'd see how awful the Flamingoes are and want to spend time with us alone."

"When are you going?" Stephanie asked. It still sounded like an awful idea to her!

"Tomorrow night at seven." Allie seemed nervous. "Could you maybe call us right before? We'll need a pep talk. You know, Steph, if you'd been here, none of this would have happened."

"I know, I know," Stephanie said. *Allie sure knows how to make a person feel guilty,* she thought.

"Don't you want to know what Brandon did?" Darcy asked.

"Brandon who?" Stephanie laughed. She got up and began to pace the room. Now this conversation was getting interesting!

"Brandon Fallow, who I thought you were madly in love with," Darcy said. "The one who didn't even show up for the party! It was just us, Dylan and Jason, and the Flamingoes."

"Really?" Stephanie said politely. "Too bad, I guess."

"Don't you even care?" Darcy asked, sounding surprised.

"Stephanie, are you all right?" Allie added.

"Definitely not." Stephanie giggled. "I'm fantastic!" she yelled. "I've met the most incredible guy in the world!"

"You met a guy!" Allie exclaimed. "So that's why you're not upset about Brandon!"

"Is he a cowboy?" Darcy asked.

"No, but he thinks I'm a cow*girl*," Stephanie told her. "I kind of tamed a wild bronc since I've been here."

"No way!" Darcy squealed.

"What's his name?" Allie asked excitedly.

"Justin. He's just so cute, you guys. And nice, too. And really easy to talk to. It's almost like he's one of you guys. But instead of being another girl, he's a gorgeous guy."

"How does he rate on a scale of one to ten?" Darcy asked.

"Eleven," Stephanie said. "No, eleven hundred."

Allie sighed. "This is so cool! Tell us everything that's happened!"

"I can truthfully say that I have been invited on an official date," Stephanie said solemnly.

"Can you believe it!" both her friends screamed at once. "When, what, where?" Darcy asked excitedly.

"On . . . a . . . covered-wagon ride!" Stephanie dragged it out for dramatic effect.

"A covered-wagon ride—that is so romantic!" Darcy exclaimed. "Oh, Steph, how perfect!"

"You don't have to tell me," Stephanie said. "I've never met anyone like Justin before. You guys, this just may be absolute, true love."

Darcy and Allie begged for more details. Stephanie couldn't help it—she had to tell them absolutely *everything!*

Next morning at breakfast Stephanie wolfed down her pancakes and asked for more.

Danny nodded approvingly. "The fresh air is giving you an appetite, Steph. That's good. I think we're all healthier since we got here. Certainly my mental health is better since I got away from the TV show."

"So's mine," said D.J. She waved at Joe, who was walking toward the corral. Stephanie made a face. She couldn't believe how much time D.J. was spending with the young cowboy. *Dad would never let me get away with that*, she thought. *He'd say it was only a silly crush. Nothing important.*

D.J.'s eyes followed Joe. She sighed heavily. "He is so great. I don't know what I'll do when we have to go home." D.J. got up. "Excuse me, Dad. Joe's going to show me how to hitch up the horses for the wagon ride." D.J. hurried after Joe toward the stable.

When we have to go home. Suddenly Stephanie lost her appetite. She hadn't even thought about going home! *It's already Tuesday. We only have two more full days left!*

No matter what her father thought, she *was* serious about Justin. She wanted to find out everything about him! And she was just getting started. How would she ever say goodbye to him on Friday?

CHAPTER
7

♦ ◄ ◆ ♦

Stephanie excused herself from the table. She had to find Justin now. She had to be with him as much as possible in the time that was left. She hurried toward Justin's cabin.

"Hey, Stephanie?" Michelle caught up to her.

"Don't you have someplace you're supposed to be right now?" Stephanie asked. What if Michelle tagged after her the whole morning?

"Yeah, but . . ." Michelle looked at her feet. "Do you remember I told you about my part in the play?"

"I remember," Stephanie said impatiently. "Annie Oakley. So?"

"I have too many lines," Michelle said. "I'm goofing up. Remember how you said you'd help me?"

"Well, sure, but—"

"Stephanie!" Just then Justin jogged over to them from his cabin. He wore cowboy boots with spurs, stonewashed blue jeans, and a T-shirt with a roadrunner on it. He looked adorable. "Listen, I got stuck making clay pots with my mother this morning," he said. "Do you want to come along?"

Stephanie thought that sounded like more fun than anything. She opened her mouth to say yes. But before she could say anything, Michelle interrupted.

"Stephanie, please, please help me! Dad said you would." Michelle folded her arms stubbornly. "And if you don't, I'll stand here and scream. Then you won't get to go anywhere with him!" Michelle pointed at Justin.

Stephanie sighed. "I guess I can't go, Justin," she said. "Unless you'd like to buy a little sister? I'd be happy to sell you one right now. Extra cheap!"

Justin laughed. "Thanks anyway. But I'll see you this afternoon, right? For the wagon ride?"

"I'll be there," Stephanie declared.

"Come on, Stephanie." Michelle tugged her hand. "I've got a million lines to learn."

Stephanie watched Justin as he joined his mother in front of their cabin. "Okay, Michelle," she said. "Let's go. If you learn your lines in a hurry, maybe I'll still have a little time left for clay pots."

Stephanie led her sister to the river. They sat under a tall cottonwood tree. From there Stephanie had a clear view of the arts and crafts cabin. Her heart leaped when she saw Justin through the window. He was shaping a pot of clay with his mother.

"My lines are highlighted in pink," Michelle said. "See how many there are?"

Stephanie flipped through the script on Annie Oakley. "My gosh, Michelle," she said in surprise. "You really do have a lot of lines."

"There's *fifty!*" Michelle said. She sounded proud of herself, but also very panicky.

"Calm down. Once we get started, it'll be easy," Stephanie assured her. She read the line that came before Michelle's. " 'You're a nice enough li'l lady.' "

"I am?" Michelle asked.

"No, silly," Stephanie said impatiently. "That's not what you're supposed to say. Say what's in the script. Now, let's try it again. 'You're a nice enough li'l lady.' "

Michelle just sat there.

"Michelle?" Stephanie prompted. "You're supposed to say 'I hope this town is big enough for all of us, boys.' "

Michelle wiped away a tear. "I just can't remember."

Stephanie looked at her little sister for a minute. She wasn't sure what the problem was. Usually, Michelle loved to perform. But now she was acting as if she didn't have a clue what she was supposed to do.

"Michelle," she began. "Just calm down. Then we'll . . ." She stopped talking. Justin had just walked out of the arts and crafts cabin.

"We'll work on this more later." Stephanie tossed the script back to Michelle. "Try not to worry. Professional actors always say that bad rehearsals mean good performances." Her eyes followed Justin.

"But you promised you'd help me." Michelle's voice trembled a little.

"Oh, I will," Stephanie said, hurrying after Justin. "Later, I will. I promise."

"Stephanie!" Danny appeared outside his cabin.

"Hi, Dad," she called.

"Were you helping Michelle with her lines for the play?"

"Um, I was, but . . . she needs a little more practice before she's ready for a rehearsal," she fudged. *Well, it's true,* she thought. *More or less. Until Michelle learns her lines better, I really can't help her.*

"Oh. Well, in that case, come up to the ranch house with me. They have some great souvenirs."

Stephanie craned her neck to see where Justin was going. She saw him heading for the corral. Jet Stream was there, pawing the ground. Usually Stephanie liked to shop for souvenirs, but today she preferred horses. "I was thinking about going riding," she said.

"Not by yourself, young lady," Danny said sternly. "You know better than that. If you want to go for a ride, I'll come with you."

Stephanie sighed and gave up. She could see

there'd be no shaking off her father that morning. "Souvenir shopping sounds like fun. Let's go." *And maybe it won't take too long,* she thought hopefully.

Danny steered her toward the souvenir stand in front of the ranch house. "I saw something I think you'll really like."

"Oh, me, too." Stephanie spotted a stack of T-shirts like Justin's, with roadrunners on the front.

"These," Danny said. He held up a pair of dyed pink moccasins. They had bright yellow and blue beading in a kitty cat design on the toes. "Aren't they cute?"

For a second Stephanie couldn't speak. They were horrible! "They sure are . . . different," she finally managed to say. She didn't want to hurt her father's feelings, but no way was she going to walk around in those moccasins! They looked like something a three-year-old would wear.

"Try them on." Danny handed her the moccasins. "I want you to have something to remind you of the trip."

So do I! Stephanie thought. *But not those moccasins!*

Stephanie had no choice. She put on the awful moccasins.

Danny beamed. "They look great, don't they?"

Stephanie nodded. She couldn't change his mind now, she realized. But, if he really wanted her to have something she liked, she could always exchange them later. In fact, she could trade them in for a roadrunner T-shirt! That way everybody ended up happy.

By the time they'd finished shopping, it was almost time for lunch, and then after lunch, Stephanie had to race to the ranch house to exchange the moccasins for the T-shirt. By then, it was time for the wagon ride. As Stephanie joined the other guests by the corral, her pulse was racing with excitement. Luke helped everyone climb into the high wagons. He kept Stephanie and Justin waiting until last. Then, finally, he helped them into their own wagon.

Stephanie couldn't believe her luck—Luke had kept his promise. Justin got to ride up front with Luke, and she got to sit next to Justin—all by themselves! Her dad and Michelle were already settled in another wagon. Joe was driving their team, with D.J. on the front seat beside him.

The old wooden wagons were beautiful. Conestoga wagons, they were called. They were the kind the settlers had driven west a hundred years ago. They had white canvas covers that reminded Stephanie of old-fashioned bonnets and huge wooden wheels with spokes.

What a super place for a first date! Stephanie thought. Next to her, Luke shifted on the rough seat, squashing Stephanie into Justin.

"Okay, you drive, kid." Luke grinned and handed Justin the reins.

"Why not let Stephanie drive the team?" Justin asked.

Stephanie gulped. *That's four horses!* she thought. *I hope they aren't four Blazes! If they are, I'll probably drive us all right off the edge of a cliff!*

"She ain't bad with horses, I'll say that for her." Luke spat a stream of tobacco juice. "Sure—why not? Do your best, little lady."

Justin handed Stephanie the reins.

"All right, Stephanie!" Justin punched the air. "Hey, we're twins today!" He pointed at her roadrunner T-shirt.

Stephanie smiled. They looked great together! Happily, Stephanie gathered up the heavy reins. The horses champed at their bits and stomped. "What do I do first?" she asked Luke.

"Slap the horses a little with the reins and yell, 'Giddyup,' " Luke said. "You guide them just like you would a riding horse—pull left or right, whichever way you want to go."

Very gently Stephanie flicked the reins on the horses' backs. Slowly the wagon creaked forward. They passed the corral and headed into the open desert.

"This is so cool," Justin said. "Don't you feel like we're in the old West, Steph? All you need is one of those long dresses and a bonnet."

"And all you need is a leather vest and a watch on a chain," she said. Justin laughed.

Stephanie lightly flicked the horses again. This time they broke out of their walk and trotted eagerly forward.

This isn't so hard! Stephanie thought. It was awesome to be steering around so much horsepower.

She spotted D.J. on her wagon, sitting up close to Joe. They were talking and laughing and not paying much attention to where they were going. She nudged Justin. "Look at Joe and D.J.," she said. "Wouldn't it be fun to wake them up?"

Luke grinned. "We can't let them win this race," he said.

"What race?" Justin asked.

"The one we're about to have." Luke lifted his hat and whooped. "Go for it, little lady!"

Stephanie slapped the horses again with the reins. The horses broke into a full gallop and pulled quickly ahead of the other wagon. D.J. looked over and waved. Joe waved his hat in the air—then he slapped the reins to hurry up their team.

But Stephanie's team went even faster. The wagon creaked and rocked from side to side. The wheels rattled and shook with every bump.

"Luke—am I going too fast?" she shouted. Maybe the wagon would fall apart, or the horses would run away!

"Not for me!" Justin yelled.

"Let 'er rip!" Luke hollered, waving his hat.

"This is a blast!" Justin yelled. "Steph—is there anything you can't do?" he shouted.

"Not anything!" she shouted back. *When I'm around you.*

The horses thundered across the flat, sandy plain. Ahead of them were the mysterious cliffs of the Indian pueblo. As they drew near, Luke and Joe signaled each other. "We'll race to that rock," Luke told Stephanie. She glanced back at D.J.'s wagon. They were way ahead—they were going to win the race!

With a whoop and a holler, Luke, Stephanie, and Justin pulled up at the rock. They had won! Stephanie and Justin high-fived each other. D.J.'s wagon pulled up next to theirs, with Joe pulling back hard on the reins. Joe smiled at them good-naturedly. "Nice driving," he told Stephanie. "You won fair and square."

A shaky voice called out. "Are you all crazy?" Stephanie turned in time to see her father climbing down from the back of the wagon. She had forgotten all about him! Danny helped Michelle climb down, then hurried over to the rest of the group.

"Stephanie—this is the worst stunt yet! I told you to use better judgment, not worse! You could have killed yourself—and Justin, you

86

should have known better, too! I warned you, Stephanie . . ."

"But, Dad," Stephanie protested. "I didn't—"

"Don't talk back! You're grounded for life!" her father shouted.

Luke put a hand on Danny's shoulder. "Hold on, Mr. Tanner, sir. It wasn't her fault. I told your daughter to race the teams."

"You did?" Danny blinked in surprise.

"Sure! Any gal who can handle horses like she can, why, I say, go for it. Besides,"—he winked at Danny—"I was right there beside her. Nothing bad would've happened."

"Oh." Danny looked embarrassed. "Then, I apologize, Stephanie. To you, too, Justin."

"That's okay," Stephanie said. But inside, she was cheering out loud. *Finally!* she wanted to shout. Finally she *hadn't* done anything wrong!

Stephanie sighed happily. Justin sat next to her on their log at the campfire. The soft firelight flickered over his face. It lit up his smile and his blue eyes. Stephanie felt tired after the long wagon ride this afternoon, but completely happy. Ever since then, her father had let up on her. Now she and Justin were actually enjoying a few minutes alone!

Well, except that the cook was still cleaning up near the chuck wagon. But Danny had taken Michelle back to their cabin, and D.J. had gone off with Joe to a star-gazing lecture.

Stephanie shivered, rubbing her arms. The fire was warming one side of her, but the night had gotten chilly on her back.

"Here, take my jacket," Justin offered.

"Thanks!" Stephanie put on Justin's black denim jacket. It was too big for her, and the sleeves hung over her hands. *I must look so, so cool*, she thought.

"My jacket looks great on you," Justin said. "Maybe you should keep it."

"R-really?" Stephanie stammered. *I can't believe I'm sitting here in a boy's jacket!* If only Darcy and Allie could see this.

But maybe she shouldn't take it. Justin might need it himself. *And what would her father say?* Stephanie turned to Justin, her eyes full of doubt.

Justin looked back at her. He seemed a little nervous. Then he leaned closer.

Was he going to kiss her? Stephanie's mind raced. What should she do? Stephanie leaned forward, too. *I'm going to be kissed for the very first time!* she screamed inside. She closed her eyes. Just then, someone tapped her on the shoulder.

CHAPTER
8

◆ ◀ ◆ ◆

Stephanie almost jumped out of her skin. Michelle was standing right beside her. Justin had moved back and was poking a stick into the fire.

"Stephanie, you've just got to help me," Michelle sobbed. "It's the play—I let the outlaws take over the town."

Stephanie couldn't believe it. This was by far the worst thing Michelle had ever done. *The most wonderful boy in the world was just about to give me my first kiss—and all Michelle cares about is her stupid play!*

Stephanie opened her mouth to yell. But then

she stopped herself. Yelling at her little sister wouldn't make a very good impression. And besides, Michelle looked more truly miserable than Stephanie had ever seen her.

"All right, Michelle," she said resignedly. "Don't cry. I'll help you."

"Well, sounds like you've got work to do," Justin said awkwardly. He started to get up.

"I . . . guess I do." Stephanie didn't know what to say with Michelle standing there. She couldn't very well ask if Justin would like to kiss her later.

"I'll see you tomorrow." Justin still sounded a little embarrassed. "Look, my mom made me promise to go bird-watching with her tomorrow. We'll be gone the whole afternoon. And then there's some lecture tomorrow night, after dinner. But maybe, after that, we could go for a walk. Late, like ten? We could meet down by the river."

"Fantastic!" Stephanie let out a sigh of relief. He wasn't mad. And a walk at night sounded as romantic as a fireside kiss!

"Night." Justin touched her shoulder.

"See you tomorrow." Stephanie watched Justin walk toward his cabin. Michelle was still crying. "Oh, stop, Michelle," she said. "I promised I'd help you with your play, and now, here I am." *Even though it's your fault I got a pat on the shoulder instead of my first kiss.* "But go wait for me in your cabin," she added. "I have to do something important first."

She just had to call Darcy and Allie! Wait till they heard what had almost happened!

In her cabin Stephanie grabbed the phone and dialed. Suddenly she stopped—this was her second call home in two days. *I'm sure it costs less to call at night,* she told herself. Besides, she wouldn't talk long.

"Hello?" Allie answered on the first ring, as if she'd been waiting for the call.

"It's me," Stephanie said. "You won't believe what happened tonight—"

"No, I won't," Allie interrupted. "How come you didn't call at seven? We're getting ready for our double date with Jason, Dylan, and the Flamingoes!"

She'd completely forgotten!

"I've never been so nervous in my life," Allie added.

"Well, try to have a good time," Stephanie said quickly. "Look, Allie. Don't let Jenni and Diana take over the conversation. Speak up! You and Darcy are funny and interesting, and Jason and Dylan should know it."

"Thanks, Steph," Allie said gratefully.

"I just called to—I mean, besides to talk about your date—I need to tell you about Justin!"

"What?" Allie asked eagerly.

"Justin kissed me," Stephanie said. "I mean, he *would* have—I'm sure he wanted to—but Michelle interrupted."

"Uh-oh. That sounds bad," Allie said. "But, Steph, you must be so excited. A guy wanted to kiss you!"

"It was very romantic." Stephanie leaned back and started to take off her boots, then changed her mind. She shouldn't get too comfortable—she couldn't talk all night. "We looked into each other's eyes in the firelight, moved closer . . . and then Michelle started bugging me about this dumb play she's in! How can I get him to kiss me again?"

"Hmm," said Allie. "I see you need some help. Here's Darcy. Let's ask her. Darcy, pick up the extension!" Allie yelled.

A minute later Darcy picked up. "Sorry, I was trying to fix my blusher." She sounded breathless. "I look like Bozo the Clown."

"Get this, Darcy," Allie said. "Justin almost kissed Stephanie."

"*Almost?*" Darcy asked.

"Michelle interrupted," said Allie. "So should Stephanie just wait for Justin to do it again?"

"I don't think so," said Darcy. "I mean, this is the nineties. You don't have to just hang back and wait for the guy to make a move. Justin made the first move, so you make the next move."

"But how?" Stephanie wailed.

In a minute or two they had a list of ten possible kissing places.

JUSTIN AND STEPHANIE'S FIRST KISS
*1. Try at the campfire again—bribe Michelle to get your Dad out of the way. *Downside:* Other people might be around and see—could be embarrassing.
2. The barn—say you need help with your horse. *Downside:* Might be too smelly in there.

94

3. If you go on another hike with *no* people around, find a romantic rock (a small one) to sit on.

4. If you go on another hike *with* other people around, find a romantic rock (a big one) to stand behind.

5. Ride double on horseback again, *away* from other people. *Downside:* Hard to turn around in the saddle to kiss. You also might bounce apart—or fall off!!

6. Go square dancing and skip away from the crowd.

7. Pretend to sprain your ankle—he'll have to put his arms around you to help you walk.

*8. Invite him to your cabin when D.J. is out on a date. *Downside:* VERY RISKY!!!

*9. ~~Ask him to meet you at the old Indian pueblo.~~ Scratch that—too scary.

10. Ask D.J. for *her* ideas.

*Note: Starred items will take extreme courage.

Stephanie looked down the list and smiled. One of them had to work! "Thanks, guys," she said. "I just wish I had more time to try these out. There's only two nights left! Two more nights—and then Justin and I may be parted forever!"

Darcy sighed. "It's so romantic."

"Yeah, but we've got to run," Allie said excitedly. "Good luck, Steph. And wish us luck, too!"

"Good luck! I'll call to find out what happened, tomorrow night—no matter what," Stephanie said. "I promise."

"Stephanie, what happened to you last night?" Danny asked the next morning at breakfast. Michelle wasn't at the picnic table yet. D.J. was sitting next to Stephanie on the bench.

Stephanie gulped down some orange juice and picked up her fork to attack the sausages on her plate. "What do you mean? I was in my cabin," she said. "All night."

"What I mean is, you promised to help Michelle with her lines for the play," Danny said. "She waited and waited in our cabin, but you never showed. Finally she fell asleep. I can't believe you let her down like that. What happened?"

D.J. leaned over and whispered in Stephanie's ear, "Don't lie!"

"Uh, I was making plans for the rest of our vacation," she told her dad. It was true—she and Darcy and Allie had made a *lot* of plans.

"Michelle was in tears." Danny shook his head. "Not good, Stephanie. I know you've got other things to do, but what about your family?"

"I'm sorry, Dad." Stephanie hadn't realized Michelle would get so upset.

Michelle walked over from their cabin. She sat down at the picnic table and stared at the pancakes Danny had piled on her plate.

"Eat, honey," Danny urged.

"I'm not hungry." Michelle shrugged. "I don't have time, anyway. I'm going Indian dancing in a second. I can dance pretty well. Even if I can't do my lines for the play."

"I could help you with them," D.J. offered.

"We all could," Danny said. "When is the play, Michelle?"

"Tomorrow afternoon," Michelle said in a little voice.

"Okay, we'll all get together after lunch and

solve the problem," Danny said firmly. "All right, Stephanie?"

Stephanie thought her father was giving her a suspicious look, as if he didn't think she'd really show up. "Fine," she said. After all, she wasn't doing anything else. Justin would be with his mother all day.

"Thanks, everybody." Michelle looked a little happier. She got up from the table and ran to join her Indian-dancing group in front of the ranch house.

"I've got to go meet Joe." D.J. got up, too. "He's giving me another calf-roping lesson. But I'll come back later to help Michelle with her lines. Okay?"

"Have a good time, sweetheart." Danny smiled at D.J. When D.J. had walked off, he turned to Stephanie again.

Uh-oh, she thought. *He's sure not smiling at me!*

Danny sighed. "Stephanie, I am really disappointed in your behavior again. You let your little sister down—badly. As of eight o'clock tonight, you are grounded."

Stephanie stared at him in horror. He couldn't

mean it! What about her walk tonight with Justin? She was supposed to meet him at ten!

"But, Dad, I promised I'd work with Michelle this afternoon!" Stephanie protested.

Danny looked stern. "Not good enough, Steph. We came here for some quality time together, and all you've thought about is your own fun."

Stephanie swallowed hard. "I know, Dad, but this is a special case. See, Justin asked me to take a walk, and it's almost a real date, and I really, seriously like him, and—"

Danny laughed and ruffled her hair. "Steph, honey—you've got lots of time ahead for serious dating! Don't worry. You'll see Justin tomorrow. In the meantime, you can think about your family. And starting tomorrow, we really *will* spend more time together."

Without another word Stephanie got up and ran to her cabin, flinging herself onto the bed. She was trying very hard not to cry. *He is so unfair!* Nobody understood what this punishment meant! She had to talk to somebody or her heart would break.

Stephanie dialed Darcy's number. "Hello?" Darcy said cheerfully.

"Darcy, the most terrible thing just happened." Stephanie tried to steady her voice.

"Steph, you sound awful!" Darcy said. "But listen—the greatest thing happened to me and Allie!"

"Really?" Stephanie forced herself to sound interested.

"Yeah! At the bowling alley last night—Diana and Jenni made total fools of themselves! They don't even know how to bowl! So they tried to talk to the guys all night, but Allie and I didn't let them. It was just like you said, Steph. Then Dylan said to me, 'Maybe just the *real* bowlers should go out sometime!' "

"That's great, Darcy." Stephanie tried to feel happy for her friend.

"So what happened to you?" Darcy asked finally.

"My dad won't let me out to meet Justin tonight." Stephanie felt a tear start down her cheek. "I'm grounded!"

"Oh, no!" Darcy exclaimed. "What about your big kiss?"

Stephanie sighed heavily. "I don't know."

"Well, I guess you can be with Justin during the day," Darcy said hopefully.

"No—starting tomorrow, Dad said I have to spend time with him!" Stephanie wiped away the tear with the back of her hand. "Oh, Darcy, this is just so terrible. I've only got today and tomorrow left with Justin. What if I don't see him alone at all?"

"Well," Darcy said slowly, "maybe you could go to your dad, tell him the truth, and get him to change his mind."

"No way," Stephanie groaned. "He's so mad at me now, he'll never listen."

"Then, I guess you have to give up your first kiss," Darcy said sadly. "What else can you do?"

"Nothing," Stephanie answered just as sadly. "There's absolutely nothing I can do."

CHAPTER
9

♦ ◢ ◼ ♦

That afternoon the Tanners gathered in Michelle and Danny's cabin to help Michelle with her lines for the play. The girls sat in a row on the bed, and Danny stood in front of them.

"I'll direct," he said. "D.J., you read the line before Michelle's first line to cue her?"

"Okay, here goes." D.J. stood up. " 'I got to admire a woman with your spirit, Annie Oakley,' " she read. She twirled an imaginary gun and glared at Michelle. " 'Don't mean I think you can outshoot me, though.' "

"Good." Danny nodded. "Okay, Michelle. Say your line."

"Um . . . 'Why, thank you, sir. I . . . Should . . .'" Michelle burst into tears. "I forgot."

"Oh, honey." Danny hugged Michelle. "There's nothing to cry about—we're all going to help you!"

Michelle snuffled. "Good. Because I'm going to look like a big red strawberry if I don't stop crying."

"Don't worry, Michelle," said D.J. "You can do this. Right, Steph?"

"Um . . . oh, yes, right. Sure."

"Okay, let's try again," said Danny. 'Don't mean I think you can outshoot me, though!' " he read, waggling his eyebrows.

Michelle burst out laughing. " 'Why, thank you, sir. Should we do a little less talkin' and a little more shootin'?"

"That's right!" Danny clapped. "Steph—you take a turn."

Stephanie helped Michelle next. They practiced for another hour. By the end of that time Michelle hardly missed any of her lines.

"You just needed to relax," Danny told her.

"Now that you know your part, you'll be fine in the performance tomorrow."

"I did it!" Michelle cried, all smiles again. "I was really okay, wasn't I?"

"You were great," Stephanie told her. She felt pretty great, herself. It was nice to do something right for a change. She tapped her father on the arm. "Uh, Dad," she said. "About tonight . . ."

"Sorry, Steph," Danny interrupted. He looked genuinely sorry, too. "I'm glad you helped your sister, but what I said before still goes. Tonight, you're grounded."

Stephanie sat on her bed that night and looked out the window. It was almost ten o'clock. D.J. was out late again—no curfews for her, Stephanie thought bitterly. Next door the lights in her father's cabin went out. Stephanie sighed. It just wasn't fair. Not only did *she* have to suffer, but poor Justin was out there alone, in the dark, waiting, and . . .

Justin! She jumped off the bed. Justin didn't know she couldn't meet him! He'd be worried, or scared that something had happened to her. She had to let him know she wasn't coming!

I'll just run out for a minute, she told herself.
*To tell him I can't keep the date. That's just being
polite—and responsible—which Dad has always told
me to be!*

Away from the ranch the night was incredibly
dark. Somehow, Stephanie managed to find the
path by the river. She walked as fast as she could
in the dim moonlight. How far was it to the Indian pueblo? She hoped she could walk it in half
an hour.

Along the river the woods were full of rustling
sounds. Stephanie's imagination started to run
away with her. What if outlaws roamed out
here? She was in the Wild West, after all!

Who-who! Who-whoooo!

Stephanie jumped and almost screamed. "Oh,
it's just an owl," she whispered. *Calm down,
Steph!* The woods ended, and she started to walk
across the desert. The sand scrunched under her
feet. At least she could see better out here—the
moonlight turned the sand into a glittering blue-
white sea. But, unfortunately, it was a big sea.
The Indian pueblo seemed awfully far away.

Well, she had to get there. Justin was waiting
for her. Stephanie picked up her pace. Finally,

after what seemed like hours, the cliffs reared up before her. She began to climb the stony path. Soon she came to the rock with the petroglyph parrot. Just beyond it, hidden by a small rise, was the pueblo. Stephanie shivered. It was a really spooky place in the dark.

"Justin will be there," Stephanie reminded herself. "We can be scared together."

She had reached the caves of the pueblo. The deep, black holes in the cliff gaped at her. Anything could hide there! Stephanie peered into the nearest cave. Where was Justin? "Justin?" she called. There was no answer, but Stephanie thought she saw a glimmer of light. *No way!* The caves were pitch black—unless, Justin was waiting inside with a flashlight. She took a step into the cave—and froze. There it was again! A patch of light . . . coming closer . . . closer . . .

It was the ghost of the Indian princess! Stephanie shrieked. She turned to run.

"Stephanie!" someone yelled.

Stephanie screamed—the ghost of the Spanish soldier! Then Justin stepped out of the shadows.

"Steph! It's me! Justin!" he said. He grabbed her arm. "You made it!"

"Justin!" Stephanie said happily. Just seeing him made her forget the horrible ghost. Justin took her hand. It was the second time! *I really feel like his girlfriend!* Stephanie thought excitedly.

"You won't believe what just happened," Justin told her. "I thought I saw something really wild . . . well . . ." he hesitated.

Stephanie couldn't believe it. "A ghost!" she nearly shouted. "I saw it, too! The Indian princess!"

"Wow." Justin's eyes grew wider. "Only I saw the Spanish soldier."

"Wow," Stephanie echoed. "This is really special. We both saw—or thought we saw—"

"The ghost of the two doomed lovers," Justin finished. "It must be some kind of a sign."

Stephanie's heart was racing. She thought so, too! "Well, I do feel kind of doomed," she said slowly. "I mean, because we just got to know each other—"

"And we have to go home so soon." Justin finished that sentence for her, too. They both laughed. "Yeah, I'll be sorry to leave here," Justin added.

They were thinking the exact same thing! *I*

know I'll miss you, *Justin,* she thought. She was much too shy to say it out loud.

"Yeah, I really got used to this place," Justin continued. "Especially the riding. Hey—want to go see our horses? I'm really going to miss Jet Stream."

"Uh, I guess I'll miss Blaze, too," Stephanie said. She and Blaze had a complicated relationship. Stephanie wasn't sure liking each other was part of it.

They walked back through the desert toward the corral. Stephanie was secretly glad to be away from the haunted pueblo. She wondered if Justin was glad, too.

In the moonlight the sand around them was cold and white, like snow. The night was very quiet. Far away an animal gave a long, slow, mournful howl. Stephanie shivered.

"It's just a coyote. They don't bother people." Justin tightened his grip on Stephanie's hand. Suddenly she was glad there were howling coyotes in the desert!

They got back to the corral pretty quickly. "Here, Jet Stream," Justin called softly. His palomino walked over to him. Justin climbed up on the fence. Stephanie couldn't see Blaze at first. Then she spotted the white stripe on his nose. "Here, Blaze!" she called.

Stephanie climbed up next to Justin and reached to pat Blaze. Blaze bumped Stephanie's arm with his nose. Stephanie ran her fingers along his neck. He had a nice soft coat. He smelled nice, too. She did like Blaze now, she realized. After all, without his help, Justin might never have noticed her.

"Will you keep on riding when you get home?" she asked Justin.

"Yeah, I think so. I've got soccer and piano lessons, but I can probably work in a ride at the stables in town sometimes. And I write for my school newspaper."

"Oh, so do I!" They smiled at each other.

"You should keep riding. You're really good at it," Justin said.

"Thanks." Suddenly Stephanie felt as if she was leaving Justin. *I wonder if we'll go back home and start doing the things we used to do and just forget all about each other?* she thought.

Justin seemed to read her mind, as usual. "I know I'll be busy when I get home, but things will be different. I won't forget you, Stephanie."

"I'll never forget you." Stephanie's voice wobbled.

Justin was looking at her very seriously. "I've never done this before," he said, leaning toward her.

This was it. He was going to kiss her! Stephanie leaned toward him, holding on to the corral rail with one hand. For just an instant she tried to remember what her kissing list said to do. Then Justin's soft lips touched hers, and she forgot all about the list. She forgot about everything except kissing him back.

"Wow," she said. She couldn't believe it—the kiss was just so nice, so comfortable, so *perfect!*

"Wow," Justin agreed with a grin. He reached over and tugged a strand of her hair. "I've got a great idea," he said. "Let's meet again tomorrow night. Maybe we could even take a moonlight horseback ride!"

Stephanie stared at him in horror. *Meet him again? She'd almost forgotten that she wasn't allowed to meet him tonight!*

Her dad was so mad already, she didn't dare

sneak out again! But how could she explain that she'd been grounded—and why? If Justin knew how selfish she'd been acting, he probably wouldn't like her anymore!

"Um," she said, "I'll try to make it tomorrow. But I'm not sure I can. In fact, I'd better get back to my cabin now." *Why did I say something so stupid?* she thought frantically. *Now he doesn't know if I want to meet him or not!*

"Well, if you're not sure . . ." Justin looked confused.

"I'll try to make it," Stephanie said. "I really will."

"Sure." Jason turned toward his own cabin. "I better go, too." He kept walking—and he didn't turn around.

Stephanie could have kicked herself! She couldn't believe what a terrible person she was. First, she'd sneaked out to meet Justin when it was forbidden. Then she couldn't make another date— and she hadn't told him the real reason why!

"Admit it," she said to herself. "You can't be honest with anyone anymore. Stephanie Tanner, when are you going to start telling the truth again?"

CHAPTER
10

◆ ◀ ◂ ◆

With a heavy heart Stephanie opened the door to her cabin. The lights were on, which meant D.J. must be back. "Deej?" she called.

"No, it's me, Stephanie." Her father stepped from behind the door. He looked worried—and very upset.

"Dad!" Stephanie stared at him in shock.

"Stephanie, do you realize what time it is?" Danny asked.

Now she was in for it! "Uh, no, Dad, I have no idea."

"It's a quarter to twelve," Danny said. "Where

have you *been?* You were supposed to be in your cabin all night."

"Well . . . uh," Stephanie's voice trailed off. She had an excuse—she was meeting Justin to tell him she couldn't meet him. But suddenly the same excuse that had sounded so clever sounded totally lame. Worse, it sounded like another lie.

"Stephanie," her father said sadly. "I don't know what to do this time. Where were you, anyway?"

"I . . . went for a walk," she said. She could tell her father didn't believe her.

Danny frowned and shook his head. "Stephanie, I have to give this some thought. I'm too tired to think about it now." He stood up and headed for the door. "But we'll talk about it tomorrow—make no mistake about it."

"Okay, Dad," Stephanie said in a small voice. "Good night."

When Danny was gone, she flopped down on the bed. She felt really bad for her father. His face was so worried and disappointed. It was *almost* enough to make her forget her first kiss. *Almost*—but not quite!

*   *   *

The strong morning sun shone on a happy, smiling Stephanie. She walked briskly toward the picnic tables and breakfast. She was totally proud of herself. Last night had been the most exciting night of her life—and she hadn't called Darcy and Allie! It had taken every ounce of willpower, but she had obeyed the rules. From now on she wouldn't do anything to get herself into trouble. She had turned over a new leaf! She was a new person. She was . . . in trouble.

"Stephanie Tanner!" Danny was marching toward her, and the look on his face was not happy.

"Good morning, Dad," Stephanie called, stalling for time. "Is something the matter?" She could see that something was very much the matter. Something more than their argument from last night.

"I just went to check on our bill," Danny said. "And what do you think I found? Charges for three and a half hours of long-distance phone calls to San Francisco! *I* don't remember making any calls home. D.J. and Michelle say they didn't make any. So, who does that leave? I don't suppose you know anything about it?"

114

Stephanie felt her face turn red. "I guess I do, Dad," she stammered. "I mean, I had to make at least one. . . ."

"I feel like an idiot, Steph," Danny said angrily. "I just chewed those cowboys out about the phone bill. I told them none of my daughters made any sneak long-distance calls."

Stephanie gulped. "I'm really sorry, Dad."

"And that's not all you've been up to," Danny went on. "I went to buy more postcards at the gift shop. And I found out you traded in your moccasins for a T-shirt. I don't get it, Steph. If you didn't like them, why didn't you tell me? Why sneak around behind my back?" He paused and shook his head sadly. "If this is what happens when you get interested in a boy, it proves my point. You're not ready for a serious boyfriend."

Stephanie just stood there, hanging her head. She had good reasons for all the things she'd been doing wrong lately. But right now, she couldn't remember what they were!

"Well." Danny looked really disappointed now. "Guess I'd better go pay the phone bill— now that I know you did make those calls."

Danny shook his head. "I'll deal with you later, Stephanie."

Stephanie ran to her cabin without breakfast. She was too miserable to eat now. She just had to talk to Darcy and Allie. She had to talk to someone who could understand her!

I'll pay for the call out of my allowance when I get home, she promised herself. *Anyway, I won't talk long.*

Stephanie dialed Darcy's number.

"Hi, Steph," Darcy answered. "What's the news from the frontier?"

"The news is the best!" Stephanie said, trying not to cry. She felt so mixed up! "And the worst, too. Is Allie there?"

"Right here," Allie said from the extension. "Good news first. What's the best?"

"Drum roll, please." Stephanie paused dramatically. "Justin kissed me last night."

"Oh, wow!" Allie practically shrieked into the phone. "You're the first of us to get kissed!"

"What was it like?" Darcy asked.

Suddenly, as the excitement of last night came back to her, Stephanie felt good again. "Well, we took a walk in the desert, and then we went to see our horses in the corral," she said. "The moon was full. . . . He said he'd never done this before, and then we kissed!"

"The desert, and horses, and a moon." Darcy sighed. "Perfect."

"But why do you sound like you have a cold?" Allie asked. "You're not crying, are you? Is something wrong?"

"My dad just *really* yelled at me for calling you guys. And for lots of other stuff I've done," Stephanie said. "In fact, I shouldn't be on the phone now, but—"

"Hey, Steph." Her father stuck his head around the door. "Come see this! The cowboys are riding bulls! They . . ." Danny's voice trailed off as he saw the phone in her hand. For a second his expression stayed the same. Then he looked terribly sad.

"Give me the phone," he said quietly.

Stephanie clicked it off. At least she could spare Darcy and Allie from hearing the argument.

"You're already grounded," Danny said slowly. "Maybe a harder punishment will make you more responsible. The cook told me he

117

needs help today at the chuck wagon. He needs someone to clean ears of corn for tonight's cook-out. I think he just found himself a helper."

About a thousand ears of corn later, D.J. stopped by to visit Stephanie. "You look like you're having a good old time," she said.

"Oh, I am. Total thrill." Stephanie tossed another ear of corn onto a giant pile.

"Dad's really mad at you," D.J. said, sitting on one of the wagon wheels.

"No kidding." Stephanie grabbed another ear of corn, yanking off the green leaves. "And I would have paid for those phone calls, too."

"That's only part of why he's mad, and you know it."

Stephanie's cheeks turned red. "I do know it," she admitted.

D.J. shook her head. "Don't you remember what I told you? Being honest with Dad is the only thing that works."

"But I can't be honest with him! I told him I really, seriously liked Justin. So now, every time I do something wrong, he blames it on that!"

"Well, that *is* why you're getting in trouble,

isn't it?" D.J. insisted. "I mean, I know Dad tries to control your life. But that's how he always is. If you want him to trust you more, you have to act *more* responsible—not go sneaking out at night, or let Michelle down, or all the other dumb stuff you've been doing. You have to work this out with him. Because Dad's not going to go away. Believe me, I know."

Stephanie put down the ear of corn and looked at her big sister.

"And you're not spending any time with the family," D.J. added. "This was supposed to be a family vacation."

"Neither are you! You're out every night with the cowboys!" Stephanie cried.

"But I've also been going for walks with Dad and Michelle, and I tell Dad what I'm doing." D.J. shrugged. "Suit yourself, Steph. But I think you'd better shape up before things get worse between you and Dad."

How could they possibly get any worse? Stephanie asked herself.

She still hadn't decided what to do by the time Danny came to collect her. It was time for the play. The cowboys had set up folding chairs in front of the ranch house. As she followed her father to a row of chairs, Stephanie felt like a prisoner. All that was missing were the handcuffs.

A bunch of little kids dressed as cowboys stood under the cottonwood tree. Michelle stood a little apart from them. She looked awfully nervous, Stephanie thought.

Stephanie leaned forward in her chair and gave her sister a thumbs-up. Michelle returned it and lifted her cowboy hat. She was wearing a red leather vest over her T-shirt and shorts, white cowboy boots, and the white cowboy hat.

"Michelle looks adorable, doesn't she?" Danny said.

"She sure does," D.J. agreed.

Luke introduced the play and everyone applauded. Then Michelle stepped forward and faced the audience. *Relax, Michelle,* Stephanie thought anxiously. *Don't forget your first line!*

Suddenly Stephanie realized that, for the first time all week, she was thinking about somebody besides herself. *Come on, Michelle!* But Michelle just stood there, staring at the audience. Somebody tittered.

120

Stephanie couldn't stand it any longer. "I'm Annie Oakley!" she hissed.

Michelle looked at her. "What?"

"I'm Annie Oakley!" Stephanie said loudly.

"Oh!" Michelle looked up. "I'm Annie Oakley!" The audience laughed.

One of the big kids swaggered over to Michelle. "This town needs a little excitement," he said.

"It does?" Michelle asked. The big kid rolled his eyes.

Stephanie made her fingers into a gun, then made a big circle in the air. *Please let her get it,* Stephanie prayed.

Michelle nodded slightly. Suddenly she turned on the other actor and drew out two toy guns she had hidden inside her vest. "Now you stop your bragging," she said, twirling the guns around her fingers. "Before things get majorly rough." The audience laughed again.

Stephanie threw Michelle another thumbs-up. Beside her, D.J. smiled at her. Michelle remembered all the rest of her lines.

"She's really good," Danny whispered

proudly. "I'm glad we helped her—all of us."
He smiled at Stephanie.

"Yeah!" Stephanie agreed. She smiled back.
Her dad might still be mad at her, but while the
play was on, they had a truce.

The play ended to wild applause. All the kids
had done a great job—but Michelle was clearly
the star. Danny, D.J., and Stephanie ran up to
her. They all shared big hugs and kisses, congrat-
ulating Michelle.

"That was a terrific job," Danny was telling
Michelle. Stephanie craned her neck around the
crowd. She'd been hoping Justin would show up
to watch. But there was no sign of him or his
mother. She hadn't seen him anywhere since the
awful scene the night before. Either he was mad
at her and avoiding her, or his mother had taken
him somewhere again. *Probably he's mad,* she
thought dismally. She turned to her older sister.

"Deej, have you seen Justin anywhere
around?"

"No, I haven't," D.J. answered.

"I saw him!" Michelle said. "Early this morning. I told him you were in big trouble with Dad,
and that you had a new job as the Corn Queen."

Stephanie stared at her in exasperation. "Where was he going?"

"He was getting in a car with his mother. I didn't ask where they were going. I'm not nosy—like some people I could name!"

"Michelle, I only have a minute!" Stephanie nearly shouted. "I have to go right back to the chuck wagon. Tell me quick—did he say anything about me?"

"Nope." Michelle smiled at her brightly. "But don't look so down. You get out of jail when we leave tomorrow."

Leave, tomorrow! Stephanie couldn't waste the valuable time they had left shucking corn! Danny was busy talking with some other parents. But she couldn't go back to the chuck wagon now! She just couldn't!

Stephanie ran to Justin's cabin. Through the window, she could see that it was empty. The beds had been stripped and the closet doors stood open—there was nothing inside. Justin and his mother weren't just out for a ride—they were gone. *Really* gone!

CHAPTER
11

◆ ◂ ◆ ◆

Stephanie pushed open the door and went inside. She couldn't believe it! Justin was supposed to stay for one more day. Now what would she do? He had gone home, thinking she didn't want to see him again! She sagged onto a bed, more miserable than she'd ever been.

"Stephanie!" Her father stepped into the cabin. "What are you doing here? Cook is waiting for you. How irresponsible can you get?" her dad demanded.

Stephanie didn't have the heart to answer him. What did it matter now, anyway?

Danny sat beside her and threw up his arms in exasperation. "There's nothing left to punish you with! I already grounded you. I guess now you're grounded until you're old enough to vote."

"Sorry, Dad," Stephanie mumbled.

Danny shook his head sadly. "Steph, what did you think this vacation was about? Our family was supposed to grow closer. But you seem to be growing farther and farther away from us! I can't believe a word you're saying anymore."

Stephanie decided to try the truth. "Okay," she said. "I'll tell you the *whole* truth. I didn't want to sneak out last night. But I'd promised to meet Justin at the pueblo, and he was waiting there alone. I had to go tell him I *couldn't* meet him."

Danny looked confused. "That almost makes sense. But why didn't you mention this before?"

"Because I thought you'd say that Justin wasn't important. That he was just a silly crush. And he's more. I really care about Justin!" Stephanie burst out crying. "And now he's gone, and I'll never see him again in my whole life! And the worst part is, he thinks I don't like him anymore."

Danny looked uncomfortable. "For heaven's sake, Stephanie. It's not as bad as that!"

"Yes, it is," Stephanie said. "He's the nicest boy I ever met. We had so much in common! I even thought you liked him, at least, I did at first."

Her father was silent for a moment. "Look, Steph, maybe I didn't give Justin a chance. But it was mostly because of the way you acted with him. Sneaking out at night and lying to me is not the way to get me to like a boyfriend of yours."

"I know," she said softly.

"I never said you couldn't like boys," Danny told her. "After all, I was interested in girls when I was your age."

Stephanie blinked. "You were?"

"Sure," Danny said. "Let's see, seventh grade—I was in love with a girl named Patricia O'Neill. She had the most beautiful red hair I'd ever seen. Of course, I never sneaked out to meet her in the middle of the night."

"But I was only being responsible to Justin," Stephanie reminded him.

"You could have told me that. The point is

that you've been dishonest with me this whole vacation."

Stephanie jumped to her feet. "Well, what about *you*, Dad?" she cried. "So much was happening to me, and I couldn't tell you the truth about any of it. I mean, Justin was becoming a real boyfriend. My first! But I couldn't tell you that! That's why I called Darcy and Allie—I needed someone to listen to me. And help me."

Danny looked hurt. "And I don't?"

"Well, when I *did* tell you the truth, you didn't even believe me. Like the wagon ride—you took my head off for racing the team, and it was Luke's idea all along. *He* treated me like a grown-up."

Danny's mouth dropped open in surprise.

"I'm sorry, Stephanie," he said.

"Sorry?" Stephanie repeated in confusion.

"Yes," said her father. "I'm still upset about your behavior. But I never meant to make you feel that you can't tell me the truth. I'm very sorry about that." He hesitated. "And, to tell *you* the truth, well, I guess I wasn't ready for you to have a real boyfriend. I have to admit it—I didn't want my little girl to be so grown up yet."

Stephanie burst into tears again. She threw her arms around her father. He stroked the back of her head. "Let's make a deal, Steph. From now on, I'll try to treat you more like the young lady you've become."

"Thanks, Dad," Stephanie said through her tears.

"And you," Danny went on, "have to promise to be honest with me. And by honest, I mean strictly honest. That means no more tricks like meeting someone to tell them you *can't* meet them. Deal?"

"Deal," Stephanie agreed.

"And now, I think we *both* have a date at the chuck wagon. Since I'm partly to blame, I'll take part of the punishment." Danny got to his feet and started for the door.

"Dad, there's one more thing," Stephanie said.

"What is it?"

"To be strictly honest, I really wanted to see Justin one more time before he left. Now that it's too late—" She hesitated. "Can you help me?"

Danny actually looked as if he was proud that she had asked. Then a troubled look came into his eyes. "I'd like to help, sweetheart," said

Danny. "But, right now, I honestly don't see how I can."

Stephanie sighed. "Me, either. Well, anyway, Dad, thanks for being honest."

Early the next morning the Tanners were on a plane headed for home. Danny was sitting with Michelle and D.J. while Stephanie sat across the aisle by herself. That was fine with her. She felt so miserable about missing Justin, she didn't care who she sat with.

As soon as they got home from the airport, Stephanie headed straight for the phone. "Dad," she yelled, "can I call Darcy and Allie and ask them to come over?"

"Sure thing, Steph." Danny shook his head. "I am really sorry about what happened with Justin. But I haven't given up trying yet. Maybe I can still help you."

Stephanie sighed. "That's okay, Dad. It's not your fault." What could her father do, anyway? She dialed Allie's number. Allie was bursting with news and couldn't wait to come over. She agreed to call Darcy and meet her at Stephanie's. Stephanie hung up and went into her room. It looked depressingly familiar. Her life was the same as it had always been, before she met Justin. He was gone. She put on Justin's coat and lay down on her bed.

A few minutes later Darcy and Allie burst into her bedroom. "Okay, what happened?" Darcy asked. "The last thing we heard was that you got kissed—and then you hung up on us!"

"I also got grounded," Stephanie said. "And Justin and I sort of had a fight, and he went home before we could make up."

"Uh-oh," said Allie. "This sounds terrible. You can write to him, though."

Stephanie shook her head. "I don't even have his address. He lives in Boston and his last name is Anderson. There're probably a thousand Andersons in Boston."

"Too bad, Steph," Allie said sympathetically.

"Come on, Stephanie, don't give up yet," Darcy urged.

Stephanie made herself smile at her friends. "But at least your love lives are going okay."

"Well, not completely," Allie said. "I mean, Jason and Dylan did ask us out again, but they asked Jenni and Diana, too! No way we're going on another group date," she declared.

"But what are you going to do, Steph?" Darcy asked.

"Nothing. There's nothing I can do," Stephanie said, sitting up. "I really think my heart is broken, you guys. I don't know how to fix that."

She missed Justin so much. She'd gotten used to talking to him, to discovering things together, to doing things together. Stephanie rolled on her back and stared at the blank white ceiling. That was what her life felt like now: a big boring white ceiling.

The next morning Stephanie felt as gloomy as ever. She felt so badly about Justin that she couldn't wait to go back to school on Monday. At least then she'd be busy, and she wouldn't be able to think about missing Justin so much. Halfheartedly, she dragged herself up to her room. She had a fuzzy idea about writing a letter to Justin. *Someday, somehow, I could find out his address. Couldn't I?*

Then the door to her bedroom opened. "May I come in?" Danny asked.

"Sure," Stephanie said.

"I have some news for you," Danny said, smiling. "I thought about what you asked, and I decided to call the ranch. I found out Justin's mom had to leave a day early for her job. And I found out something else—her phone number. I called, and one thing led to another, and—" Danny whipped a sheet of paper from behind his back. "And this fax just came in."

Stephanie sat up, her heart hammering. *A fax?* "Who's it from?" she asked.

"Justin." Her dad handed it over.

Stephanie grabbed the sheet and kissed it. Then she remembered her dad was watching. "You didn't read it, did you?"

Her father smiled at her. "That's part of our new deal, remember? I'm trying to treat you like an adult now. And one adult would never read another adult's fax."

"Of course not, Dad. Sorry I asked." Stephanie looked down at the paper. Her hand was trembling a little.

Dear Stephanie,
You won't believe what happened?! Sorry I

132

disappeared. My mom had to leave a day early. We didn't even get to say goodbye! I didn't have your address, but then your dad called my mom, and I got your fax number!

Stephanie felt relief wash over her. He wasn't mad at her at all! She continued to read.

I know we were only together for a week, but it was really special. Did you think so, too? Here's my address for the next time you're in Boston—ha-ha. I guess it's only three thousand miles to Boston from San Francisco. But seriously, I might come for a visit someday. That is, if you want me to. Please write and tell me.

Your friend,
Justin

"Good news?" Danny asked.

"The best!" Stephanie beamed. "Dad—thanks for doing this for me. Thanks for calling Justin's mom and . . . and *everything!*"

"See? We can talk things through—honestly." Danny ruffled her hair.

Stephanie hesitated. "Dad, since we didn't get to ride together much at the ranch, why don't we go to Fun City this weekend?" she asked. "We could do all the rides—even the merry-go-round. The whole family!"

"It's a date," he agreed happily. "As Michelle would say, 'Yippeeyioh-kiyay!'"

FULL HOUSE™
Michelle

#1: THE GREAT PET PROJECT

#2: THE SUPER-DUPER SLEEPOVER PARTY

#3: MY TWO BEST FRIENDS
(coming mid-June)

Based on the Hit TV Series!

Available from

A MINSTREL® BOOK

Published by Pocket Books

OUTSTANDING AND UNIQUE!
INCREDIBLE! ELITE!
THEY'LL SWEEP YOU OFF YOUR FEET!
GO PATTI! GO CASSIE!
GO LAUREN! GO TARA!

THE PAXTON CHEERLEADERS ™

GO FOR IT, PATTI!

☆

THREE CHEERS FOR YOU, CASSIE!

☆

WINNING ISN'T EVERYTHING, LAUREN!

☆

WE DID IT, TARA!

☆

WE'RE IN THIS TOGETHER, PATTI!

A MINSTREL® BOOK

Published by Pocket Books   1021-03